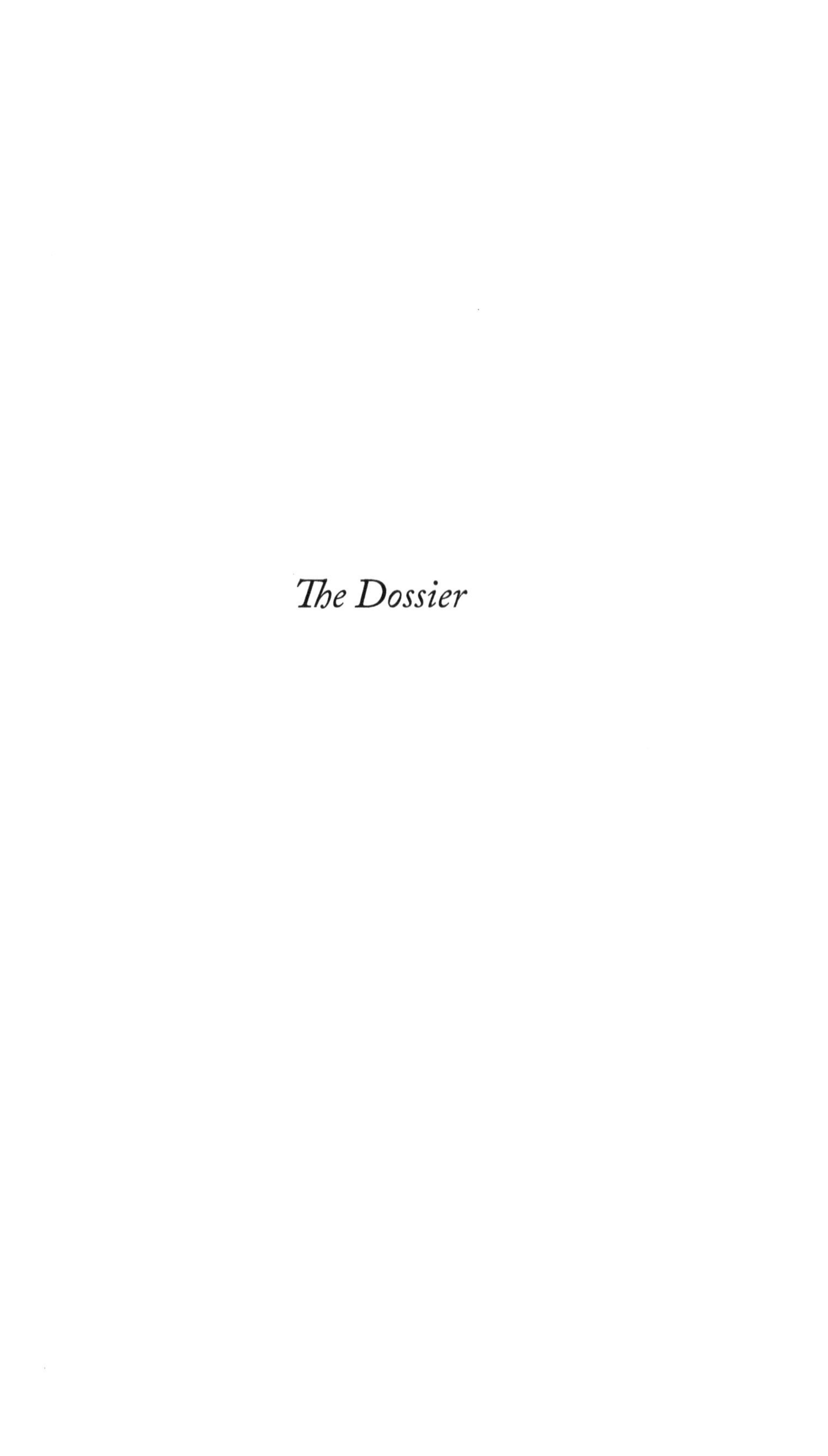

*The Dossier*

Cover: "Laura" Linda Berrón, mixed technique, 2016
Design: Michael Godeck


chiringapress@gmail.com

ISBN 978-1-61012-038-8

# *The Dossier*

Linda Berrón

Translation by
Mayela Vallejos Ramírez and Edward Waters Hood

Chiringa Press
Seguin, Texas 2018

## Contents

*The Dossier*

# A Postmodern Revision of the Don Juan Myth in *The Dossier* by Linda Berrón

Mayela Vallejos Ramírez

*-Colorado Mesa University-*

Right from its first pages *The Dossier* is an enigmatic and audacious novel with ironic and sarcastic language in which gender power struggles, relations between couples, the seduction of erotic love, and repressed desire are highlighted. First published by EDUCA (Editorial Universitaria Centroamericana) in 1989, it has been republished twice, by Editorial Mujeres (1995) and InÉditor (2009). It can be affirmed that, with this novel, Linda Berrón consolidated her novelistic career, since her first two books were short story collections. The novel's publication elicited serious, positive reviews in magazines and national newspapers, foretelling its resounding success, not only for the themes it deals with, but also for the mastery with which the plot is constructed. Amelia Chaverri's comments on the back cover of the first edition rightly point out how the peculiar manner in which Berrón manages information and suspense entraps the reader from the first pages, since "with these elements the author displays her ingenuity and great sense of observation to create a unique character through whom she captures a mosaic of reflections on love, where the machista cultural paradigm is skillfully outlined." Therefore, the reader finds him or herself faced with a novel that reflects, to such a great degree, the sociological, psychological, and cultural aspects of love relations in Costa Rican and Hispanic American societies in which women are considered an object of masculine desire. Arnoldo Mora emphasizes that the originality of this text is rooted in its "manifestations of a Don Juanesque machismo, which the author situates within the urban petty bourgeoisie that is tied to the state bureaucracy" (*Suplementos*, 7).

Without doubt, the theme of Don Juan has been constant in Spanish literature. Traits of this enigmatic and captivating character, who receives his complete form in José Zorilla's famous *Don Juan Tenorio*, can be found in early peninsular texts like Fernando de Rojas's *La Celestina*. However, the Don Juan archetype has not been as common or important in Latin American as in Spanish literature. With close scrutiny, it is possible to find traces of this fascinating character type in Latin American letters, but treated in a different fashion. For this reason, Linda Berron's novel *The Dossier* is so relevant to this discussion: The main character, Andrés, is a kind of modern-day "Don Juan," but one examined from a female gaze through a neutral narrator who at the same time introduces us to Elida, the woman who is going to change Andrés's life completely by taking ownership of the male role and questioning the patriarchal roles established by society.

In this fascinating novel, the writer takes on the task of playing with a series of patriarchal myths and concepts in order to subvert them and, in doing so, offer us an ironic and provocative treatment of the roles played by both genders in society. At first glance, this novel deals with a forty-year-old man who has decided to create an archive to keep a record of his amorous conquests. Andrés has always considered himself to be a chosen one because of the luck he has had with the opposite sex. Having reached maturity, he feels the strange need to record his conquests because his memory is beginning to fail him and he is mixing them up in his mind.

The revision of masculine myths in contemporary works by women is important because it reveals a fundamental trait of this new literature. The appropriation of old myths allows us to break with cultural patterns that limit and degrade the image of women. Therefore, the reevaluation of patriarchal values found in these texts allows us to observe a commonplace event or a philosophy rooted in the idiosyncrasy of a people from another perspective and, at the same time, to redefine the social and cultural concepts that patriarchal society has imposed throughout human history. The rewriting of mythical texts is a way of rediscovering that image or identity that circumstances have obligated women to renounce in order to accept what society has created for them, which only diminishes their own lives. Therefore, to recover the lost identity, women must break with certain expectations that have been imposed on them. This rebellion is shown through the appropriation and the destruction of the myths that have been created around them in order to achieve a real change.

Here, specifically, we make reference to the Don Juan myth, which constitutes an ideological inheritance from the patriarchal and machista world that idealizes the figure of the strong, dominant, and womanizing man over the fragile, submissive, and passive woman. In *The Dossier*, the mythic figure of Don Juan is developed from a particularly feminine angle, because the treatment given to the protagonist, the modern-day Don Juan, deconstructs the masculine image while constructing a feminine one. The intertextuality present in this work includes parody, allusion, and irony, not only in relation to the Don Juan myth, but also to that of Cinderella. Both texts serve to frame the novel, because the intertextuality functions in it as an agent that generates the new text which emerges piece by piece on several levels, because the novel is developed in a fragmentary fashion. The lives of both characters are presented in intercalated chapters that have a point of convergence when the couple has their brief love encounter, only to begin again a separation that sets both on totally separate paths. However, the encounter has left an indelible mark on each of the protagonists, signaling the destruction of one and the creation of another.

In this manner, the process of demythification of these characters is carried out through the comparison and contrast between the mythic figure of Don Juan and the fundamental role played by women in this process. The masculine character is presented to us in the first chapters of the novel as a twentieth-century Don Juan. Andrés, the protagonist, alludes to all his love conquests and his desire to perpetuate the sexual thrills he receives from those amorous encounters through the creation of his own personal dossier. He especially wants to do this because he has begun to notice that the images and memories of his innumerable lovers have begun to intermingle and sometimes he is not even sure whether they are a product of his imagination or that those women really existed: "He was thirty-three when the real women became muddled in his mind, and when they started to fade into the distance. He began to lose track and to forget details." This retelling of his love affairs allows us to penetrate his most intimate feelings and to recognize the psychological, social, and cultural factors that make him an insecure person: a sense that his own self negation has produced in him, which leads him on a search to overcome the state of solitude in which he finds himself, without being able to overcome it. These are characteristics that we have to infer in the donjuanesque characters of Tirso de Molina, José de Espronceda, and José Zorilla, because these earlier figures represent an archetype that reveals the complexity of a human being lacking a maternal figure, which, to a certain degree, determines his incapacity to fully develop as a person. Besides, his secure economic condition and social position turn him into a spoiled and capricious child who is used to getting what he wants, but we never know for sure the reasons that led this man to his solitude and frivolity.

The character Andrés, although he does display a similar kind of mental orphanhood, coming from a dysfunctional family—a machista father who, in addition, hit his wife—his ability to incorporate himself in society takes on a somewhat different aspect. Andrés is a productive man in society and highly private in his relationships with his own gender. In a short period of time, he learns not to brag about his love conquests because of the envy it elicits in his male friends and also because he is convinced of the importance of discretion and the anonymity of his numerous lovers: "Protecting the 'reputations' of his lovers was of vital importance; it was a long-term erotic investment. It was important for them to feel safe, protected by his chivalrous silence." In this, Andrés differs from the mythical Don Juan, who relishes in bragging about his multiple romantic conquests in front of his friends and even places bets on them before carrying them out. This is, perhaps, because the mythic figure is more in love with himself, and his pleasure does not reside in sexual relations, but in the status of seducer that makes him appear superior to his friends and, by extension, to all other men. On the contrary, Andrés does not see his ability to seduce women as something special: "He never wondered whether all men were as lucky or if he, alone, had been chosen."

Bragging about his seductions is not an alternative for this modern-day "Don Juan." For Andrés, his personal eroticism is more important. Although women continue to be the instrument that provides him with sexual satisfaction, his memory is what really gives him greater satisfaction. "He stored away personal experiences for his fantasy alone. Every woman left a double in his imagination, and it was that double that often brought him the greatest satisfaction." Hence his need to open the dossier, because he is afraid to lose his memories and, as a result, his capacity to fantasize and satisfy his physical and mental needs. Thus, the dossier acquires the character of a confessional diary through which he can perpetuate his memories and satisfy his role as a seducer. Curiously, keeping a diary is a practice that traditionally has been attributed exclusively to women. However, in this text it is transformed into an element of the male economy—the economic power and control that men have in society—and actually allows us to see the man who is hidden behind the mask of cynicism and frivolity.

In contrast with the masculine figure, we encounter the character of Elida, who finds herself in an important moment of transition in her life. She has just ended a seven-year relationship with Federico, one of her university professors, who was many years her senior. This divorce has left her with a feeling of emptiness because she realizes that her dream, of being a Cinderella, is a fantasy. She dreamt of a Prince Charming who would rescue her from her monotonous existence and offer her a new life full of happiness and pleasure: "She entered that relationship with Federico hoping to find the ideal man: a powerful, tender man who would take control over her life, a man as asexual as possible, some kind of intelligent and sensitive eunuch, one capable of overcoming his contradictions and salvaging love." She thought she had found that ideal man in her old history professor, who she set about to seduce and conquer. This worked until the day that Federico let himself be carried away by his instincts and he possessed her in a rather violent fashion. She awoke from her dream and realized that, in the end, all men are the same: "She told herself—as if she had known and accepted it all along—that she could not expect Federico to break the mold of his gender: he was a man." Forgiving him, she agrees to marry him because she is convinced that she has a relevant role to play in that man's life. This is the result of the feminine struggle, which society usually ends up winning, because the principles that are inculcated in the feminine economy from the early, formative years are deeply ingrained in female behavior. Therefore, women end up accepting that they are inferior, receptacles, seducible, deceivable, impregnable, and subject to ridicule. As Cixous points out, by accepting these concepts, women are negating their capacity to discover who they are: "We've been turned away from our bodies, shamefully taught to ignore them, to strike them with that stupid sexual modesty; we've been made victims of the old fool's game: each one will love the other sex. I'll give you your body and you will give mine" (885).

By breaking with the fantasy of fairy tales, Elida realizes that her body has really never belonged to her because both bodies always belonged to Federico. In the solitude of her apartment, she realizes that she is just a shadow of herself, and she thinks that she would love to invent another "self," one that would be capable of overcoming the crisis in which she finds herself. However, she realizes that she has lost the ability to fantasize, which perhaps she never had. Women, as Cixous notes, are passive, silent beings created only within masculine fantasies. Therefore, women do not really have their own voice with which to express their own feelings; their world has been constructed within the parameters of masculine economy, which, instead of representing feminine needs, represents masculine ones. The capacity to create does not exist for women because language does not belong to them. Elida's urgent desire to howl results from this inability to know how to represent herself: "... and then a primitive desire to howl springs from her tiny nucleus. She stops, she howls, and she feels great." Elida has taken the first step towards her freedom and the creation of an authentic "I" that belongs to her. Cixous asserts that sexual repression and the inability to know one's own body is what prevents women from discovering themselves. Therefore, women should start with their sexuality, discovering their own bodies can help them break through the patriarchal barriers that have oppressed them for centuries.

At that precise moment, Andrés appears in her life. It amazes her that she was able to reject his invitation: "She undressed and got into bed. Something about her attitude towards men had changed. She noticed it that night. The solitude that she had experienced recently had, for the first time, placed her on the same level with men..." Her second encounter with Andrés is crucial for her awakening because she assents to have relations with him because she has taken control of the situation. Unlike her first sexual encounter with her ex-husband, this time she does not allow Andrés to take her by force. Andrés, frustrated by seeing his prey escape, assumes a totally passive attitude, one which is more like what is expected from the woman and which takes him back to his first sexual encounter, which was with the prostitute who devoured, frightened, and humiliated him. Elida, who is curious about the change, decides to indulge herself, to enjoy the pleasure of initiating relations with Andrés: "Over and over again, she relived what she had felt at that moment—surprise, delight, even her eyes were captivated by his spell, an immobilized man, a statue just for her, a present, she the protagonist, the possessor, the dominant one, the absolute owner of his desire,..." This relationship takes an unexpected direction for both of the protagonists because Elida discovers the key she was searching for to free herself from the myths that society imposes upon women: "Elida felt no hostility towards him or sadness for him. She had already given up on her idea of a dream man, because he does not exist. She had also renounced the impossible job of turning a man into her perfect prince. Now, she could only try to understand and accept men as they are, as they come, like Andrés."

Her encounter with Andrés reveals to her the world's realities, and not only does she break with her own myths and stereotypes, but also with the masculine ones: "A long time ago, when she would see a grown man cry, it was heart wrenching. But then, when she learned that men cry just as much and almost as often as women, it no longer made an impression on her." The relationship between Elida and Andrés greatly favors the young woman, who, unlike Andrés, can find herself and discover that her body, mind, and life belong to her independently of masculine desire. While Andrés starts to dissipate, Elida begins to take control of herself. In his desire to keep her, Andrés even breaks his rule and asks her to stay and sleep with him, but she no longer needs the protection of a masculine figure to feel she is a self-realized person in this world: "Though she was still Elida, she was herself in a different way." Elida exits Andrés's life forever, leaving him with a tremendous sense of emptiness: "Andrés felt lonelier than ever." And he recalled the interminable list of women who one day had begged for the love he now begged from Elida, who, master of herself, was distancing herself from him: "Elida felt an immense desire to howl, but she smiled, a new smile that changed her face, and she no longer needed to be younger or more beautiful to be happy, because she could be herself no more than she was at that moment, and that is the greatest beauty and the greatest happiness,..." Upon returning home, ironically, Elida wondered, "...what would Andrés think if he knew that he was going to be the first entry in a love diary that she planned to inaugurate that very night?"

As can be appreciated in this text, the roles change slowly as the plot thickens. Elida is able to supplant Andrés and turn herself into a kind of female Don Juan. The interesting thing about this novel is that it shows to us a woman's ability to recognize that she is a thinking being who does not need the masculine figure to validate herself. Elida has learned that she does not need a man to find a place in society. She has liberated herself from the patriarchal chains in order to begin a new life. In sum, this type of text shows how contemporary feminine works break with patriarchal models in order to create a much more positive literature, a literature that lets us measure the values of the past in contraposition with modern ones and allows for a reformulation of a new reality for women.

*Translated by Edward Waters Hood*

Texts Cited:

Berrón, Linda. *El expediente*. San José: Editorial Mujeres, 1995.

Cixous, Hellen. "The Laugh of Medusa". *Signs*. Trans. Keith Cohen and Paula Cohen. vol. 1, no. 4, 1976, pp. 875-893.

Mora, Arnoldo. "*El expediente* de Linda Berrón." *Suplementos los libros*. San José. 1989.

# *The Dossier*

**That unexpected tension** had all started with the metal file cabinet. Still somewhat asleep, he got up and opened the upper drawer in his closet. He took out an old black briefcase and placed it on the table. Tenderly, he traced a slow spiral in the white dust. He rarely opens it, except when he wants to reconcile himself with life. Tonight is one of those occasions. He opens it and nostalgically contemplates his old love offerings: a treasure of memories, the majority rescued from the destructive impetus that usually accompanies the lack of affection of spurned women.

He caresses the photographs; he remembers them one by one, smiling. He reads their inscriptions, inhaling the light fragrance of the dry flowers, embroidered handkerchiefs, and the small articles of intimate clothing that had been conveniently misplaced. He closes his eyes and caresses his skin with curly braids of hair. He kisses drawings, poems, red kisses, letters of love and hatred, imploring and threatening letters: that fascinating concoction of feminine desire.

And Andrés, standing before his imaginary chorus of lovers, facing the repeated whirlwind of faces and voices that surround him calling his name, finally feels he has been affirmed, justified, and satisfied.

He closed his briefcase and went back to bed. Armed now with the countenance of an Olympic athlete, he recognized around him the presents and rejections with which so many women had inhabited his world: glass and porcelain figurines, pictures, books, wine glasses, ceramic objects, ashtrays, a hexagon-shaped mirror, a white rug of llama wool—in every corner, love's sweet sediments.

The small narcissistic wound of that evening now healed, Andrés falls asleep, with his hand gently resting on his masculinity.

# Chapter One

## *The Dossier of Ecstasy*

The metal file cabinet had brought back to Andrés tormenting memories of a school exam. He bought it to hold his files. Despite his initial euphoria, he realized that it was only the beginning of a very ambitious plan that had obsessed him for months. He had always been successful with women. He never wondered whether all men were as lucky or if he, alone, had been chosen.

From a collector's instinct that had accompanied him since childhood, he kept a mental record that began with his scrawny cousin who had touched his private parts behind the dining-room door when he was seven years old.

Time passed, and he kept accumulating conquests in his memory. At first, he enjoyed bragging in front of others, especially his friends and colleagues who looked at him with envy. Later, the envious glances of others interested him less than the amorous eyes of the women he seduced. And he stopped bragging. He stored away personal experiences for his fantasy alone. Every woman left a double in his imagination, and it was that double that often brought him the greatest satisfaction.

He was thirty-three when the real women became muddled in his mind, and when they started to fade into the distance. He began to lose track and to forget details. He mistook names and places. It took him a few more years to decide that the time had arrived to take the matter more seriously, more scientifically, if possible.

When he bought the metal file cabinet, he had just turned forty. He was, without question, a good-looking man. A calm, physical maturity had left several lines on his face, particularly along the edges of his mouth and forehead. His physique and face had achieved that special harmony in which everything fits perfectly. His profound and leisurely gaze complemented the supple and decisive movements of his body. His voice and hands were equally skilled at caressing. An explosive combination of sweetness and coldness gave him that touch of ambiguity that women very often find enchanting.

It was difficult for him to finally decide to start from scratch, but it would have been impossible for him to create files for so many women that had loved him. In many cases, he only remembered minor details, a few exciting, entertaining memories at most, some of them bitter and even humiliating.

*"The first one, for example. The first time, I didn't even realize I had done it. The prostitute took her clothes off in front of me, devouring me with lascivious eyes that frightened me. When I felt I was inside her, it was over. She threw me out of her room with a smile that was both indulgent and sarcastic. But the worst humiliation was that she refused to take my money, why did she do that? One of the most important details that I had carefully prepared was to pay for the service: to pay for sex with a woman, to have that feeling of power, to know that you are a man. Her pimp was waiting for me at the door with a similar smile. The son-of-a-bitch was one of my father's friends. I guess they had conspired to humiliate me. Keep your money for next time. And they laughed. Of course, there were many other times. I felt powerful when I negotiated the price with them and handed them the money.*

*It didn't take me long to overcome the bondage of that machista prejudice that works against us. Why should I pay if I can get it for free?* Au contraire, *I have paid a couple of debts with some amorous afternoons to get myself out of trouble. That's why I say that, when it comes to business, I'd rather deal with women, you can always work out a deal in bed.*

*They've only tried to charge me more on two occasions, demanding endless sessions from me that bordered on possessive blackmail.*

*The only time I have been rude to a woman was on one of those occasions. It might sound crazy, but I still feel bad when I remember her crying.*

*I believe that, at heart, I'm just a big fool."*

Sometimes pleasant memories from the past would return a woman to his arms, a weapon against the inertia of time. In such cases, he could rekindle in the present forgotten pleasures from the past.

It would be impossible to recover them all! He thought, with a deep sigh. The first step of his plan was to acquire that moss-colored letter-sized metal file cabinet. He also bought hangers for the fifty files he would use to start his classified-love enterprise.

His zeal to document every single one of the inaugural details would force him to open the dossier well ahead of time. It was not wise to wait until his deeds were consummated, because he ran the risk of forgetting important early details, which generally are the most interesting ones. Besides, that would be helpful in the event two or more romances presented themselves simultaneously. That had not happened often in the past few years, as he had succumbed to a kind of serial monogamy, but there had of course been a few cases and he knew that it was risky to rely on his memory. In those circumstances, the mixing up of names, affectionate nicknames, things said, and places visited had been detected by the cleverest women, creating for him more than a few difficulties. And that really inconvenienced him, because, there was one thing about Andrés: the courteous principle to satisfy, as far as possible, the excessive female need to posses. He even became an expert of peripheral vision, allowing him to admire other women without his companion noticing anything, because he realized that most women detest that kind of voyeurism.

After arranging the files, he sat down in a ritualistic manner in front of the metal file cabinet as if it were an inspirational totem, and he set about to create a classification system. The simplest arrangement would be to place the folders in alphabetical order: last names first, then their names. And to break it down even further, it would be better to include middle names. The concept of excluding middle names, as in some telephone directories, seemed an imperfect system to him. He continued to meditate. There was something about the plan that he did not like. Besides being overly simple, and the easy way always ends up being harder, even in matters of classification, it was not a very secure system, and it could even be dangerous if it fell into the wrong hands. One of the things he had learned over the years was the need for absolute discretion. Protecting the "reputations" of his lovers was of vital importance; it was a long-term erotic investment. It was important for them to feel safe, protected by his chivalrous silence. They all knew that his mouth was shut tighter than a tomb and that no vulgar comment, not even their names, would come out of him. If the situation were to present itself, he would deny ever having met them. Although, given his record, probably no one would believe him. In this way, however, they would confirm their conjectures.

That deceptive tactic had allowed him to enjoy delicious situations in which, on the occasion of a party or other social events, he ran into several of his former lovers chatting away with one another. Here, Andrés had hit upon one of Picasso's favorite pastimes.

However, if for some unfortunate circumstance his dossier were to fall into the hands of some unscrupulous person, the word would spread quickly—within such a small circle—and his lovers would become the object of scorn or jokes. In the future, many women would avoid getting close to him, probably the ones he liked the most. Because, there were the others, the idol worshipers, the ones who even preferred to be part of the harem of a man reputed to be magnificent than enjoy exclusive rights to an average one.

And he didn't even want to imagine what would happen if his file were to fall into the hands of a scorned woman.

*"Like Julia, what a woman, a female so sweet and tender, then suddenly she turned into a bitch. I've never understood that ability women have to go from love to hatred so quickly and with equal intensity. They seem to be incapable of discernment, of keeping things in perspective. When they do something, they do it with body and soul, heart and mind, without thinking. It's like an emotional totalitarianism.*

*I learned it first hand with Julia. When she found out I had been lying to her, that I no longer loved her, as she would say, she devoted herself to making my life miserable. As if seeing me suffer made her suffering more bearable. She even sent anonymous letters to my place of work, to my fellow workers, to my boss, and she went everywhere saying bad things about me.*

*The worst part was the photos she took of a married woman I was seeing at the time. She threatened to show them to the woman's husband. She wouldn't have gotten anywhere with that, but I didn't want to get into that situation. I had to go back to her for a while, to calm her down. Violent separations, which some of my friends who had seen Fatal Attraction recommended, weren't my style. I've never hit a woman, not even when I was drunk, despite the example my father set for many years. Since then, I've been a lot more careful. I acquired the almost unconscious habit of finding and keeping to myself some compromising information with which to defend myself in case someone tries to blackmail me.*

*After all, life has its risks. That's the way women are, you can either take them or leave them. And of course, I take them.*

# Chapter Two

## *Portrait of a Love Affair*

He put aside the memory of Julia and continued to reflect on the dossier. He had stopped looking for a more secure filing system. He could introduce some variations, for example, he could just use their initials. Each file would have three letters, something that appealed to him a great deal because he had been fond of the number three, perhaps because he was born on the third day of the month. Nonetheless, the three-letter system was too rigid, and no doubt it would result in many confusing repetitions. It dawned on him to add the first vowel of each name after the initial letter. Then there would be three syllables. Too elementary, he thought. Suddenly the solution came to him: he would assign a number to each vowel. This felicitous combination of letters and numbers seemed, in a certain futuristic way, brilliant to him.

He took pen and paper and started writing. The letter A would be a 3; the E, a 7; the I, a 5; the O, an 8; no, that's a giveaway, besides, 8 is an even number, it'd be better for the O to be one, and the U can be nine. For example, Rosa would be R1. He smiled, amused with himself because it sounded like a kind of French automobile.

He tried out the system with fictitious names, because he did not want to remember the names of his old lovers even for this little trial run.

He wrote:

Rosa Molina López= M1 L1 R1

Once he had finished writing, it seemed a little monotonous, so he decided to add slashes: /M1 / L1 / R1 /. That's it. The name codes would be placed on folder tabs.

For a while, he savored the satisfaction of having achieved a certain degree of systematization, but it was short lived. He thought about how easily he forgot names. Sometimes he could remember a small detail, a strategic mole for example, but not a name. Besides, there had been instances when he did not even know the women's first names, much less their last names, either because of the urgency of those situations, or because he did not care about their names, or because they preferred to remain anonymous.

He wrote down other possible categories that could serve as a system to catalog his materials, for example age, with years and months. That won't work with women, he told himself. Place, date, and hour in which the deeds were consummated? And what if they weren't consummated? Would he include such cases in his dossier? Code the addresses? No, none of the alternatives satisfied him, none of them offered the possibility of multiple combinations offered by first and last names.

He crossed them out with a big X and, somewhat upset, thought that he would have to make a slight change in his way of doing things in order to find out the first and last names of the women he seduced. And besides that, he would have to write this information down immediately to protect it from the ravishes of oblivion or indifference.

He took another sheet of paper and wrote: II-Internal Organization of the Dossier. Some general information was essential. He drew a series of dashes: Age, Race, Virgin (yes or no), Star Sign, Nationality, Marital Status, Number of Children (if any), Contraceptive Method of Choice, Address and Telephone Number (both in code, for example, with the four cardinal directions backwards and adding a number to each digit of a telephone number); Occupation, Place of Work (if any), Rough Estimate of Personal Income, Education, Color and Length of Hair, Color and Shape of Eyes, Kind of Lips, Birthmarks or Distinguishing Characteristics such as moles, scars or tattoos; Height and Weight; Waist, Chest, and Hip Size ... He paused. How am I going to get these last three statistics? He wondered. He could not imagine himself using a measuring tape. Suddenly it occurred to him that it might be useful to draw a female body on each file, with both frontal and rear views. This idea led him to consider the wisdom of learning how to translate tactile sensations into inches. In that way, he would be able to deduce a woman's size by grabbing her around the waist. Then, it was just a matter of writing down the numbers on the female template of her file. He became sad when he thought a little about how poor an indicator of female curves and forms a precise measurement was. He would try to compensate for this limitation in his drawings of their body shapes.

He rejected, with a duplicitous smile, the typical obscenity of men's rest rooms. Photographs, which were inevitable, would be placed in the black briefcase where he kept his trophies. That was safer.

Unintentionally, he entertained again the doubt that a moment before—like a bad memory—he had tried to put out of his mind. He could not ignore the problem. And what if the deeds were not consummated? If he opened a file right from the very first romantic interludes, he could not know for sure whether or not it would turn out right for him. Although he rarely failed, the idea of looking foolish for having opened a nice file for nothing upset him. But since he was a positive person, or at least tried to be one—after all, it's just as hard to be a positive person as a negative one—he preferred to believe that even in the worst situation he could learn something. He would include his fiascos, and what is more, he would analyze them.

Discounting the dark possibility of failure, he continued working on the internal organization of the dossier. After general information, physical traits, and place of residence, he thought that he should include more subtle information regarding personality traits. He wrote down what came to mind: happy, serious; fiery, frigid; bright, dull; romantic, practical; timid, gregarious; calm, nervous; quiet, talkative; likes and dislikes; personal hobbies; special quirks. He continued without much enthusiasm: political affiliation, religion, what else?

He questioned the need for this kind of information for such an open-minded and tolerant person as himself. He had never halted a conquest for ideological reasons. At any rate, he had decided to execute this matter in a rational manner, and he had to take into consideration these aspects that could have some relevance and importance, even if not in an explicit way. He recalled with nostalgia special moments when he and his lovers had held the same beliefs. Those moments had been no less beautiful for their ephemeral nature.

He settled in his chair and, regaining a practical tone and the pleasure of rationality, he thought that those categories would allow him to compare cases, carry out some statistical cross-studies, develop hypotheses and reach a greater knowledge of himself and of his women; they would also help him to come up with new strategies for future ventures.

The development of each episode would come next. Each affair was similar but unique. In all of them the same elements came into play, but the almost infinite possibilities of chance made each liaison an authentic adventure. For that reason, there was no room for closed categories. He would write freely, allowing magic to take over, scrutinizing and recreating the most beautiful moments.

He experienced an exciting emotion when he reached this section of the file: so many fleeting experiences rescued from the oblivion of forgetfulness. The physical certainty of his dossier would allow the ephemeral moments of pleasure to triumph over the malignant relativity of reality.

He decided to divide each story into three parts. "Encounter" would be the first part, probably the most important one. He would describe how and where he met her, and what techniques of seduction he employed in his approach. The initial game of seduction.

"Affair" would be the second part. The place where he would document the dirty deeds. Where, how, and when they took place. How he would savor every minute detail of each amorous encounter. He would fill the paper with passionate images and sensations, caresses, words, moans, awkward moments, world records and, sometimes—let's face it—big disappointments.

The last part would be called "Breakup." The most delicate part: endings come in many shades. Coldness and objectivity must be observed here. Things to take into consideration, he wrote: Length of Affair; Technique Used to Get Rid of Her, if it came to that; Other Endings; Friends or Enemies; Open or Shut Case; Final Balance.

*"Other endings... There was no one like Raquel: twenty-four goodbye letters, that electrified writing style, as if she were possessed, in a state of desperation, she said goodbye to me over a period of eight unforgettable months.*

*Each breakup was followed by the exciting anxiety of a reconciliation, a new beginning, the frenzy which exploded within our bodies, a victory over oblivion and routine existence.*

*Raquel, an eternal farewell, the hallucinatory fulfillment of a longed-for, postponed desire, distancing herself from her friends, lovers, work, home, places. The compulsive repetition of a distant farewell, primordial and remote.*

*Her face never beamed more brightly than then; her kisses were never so sweet. She never loved with so much fury as when she said goodbye forever.*

*Twenty-four letters, a white lace bow tied for the last time. The last letter, the final goodbye, it didn't say it directly; it just described the sad medieval tale of the simians:*

*Monkey nature is such that, when they have twins, they love one of their offspring very much but hate the other one. For this reason, if a hunter ever chases the mother monkey, she cradles the one she loves the most against her chest, protecting it with her arms, and she carries the one she dislikes on her back. And it's precisely for this reason that, when she tires of trying to flee on two legs, she discards the one she loves and continues on her way with the one she detests on her back.*

*I wonder which one I was for Raquel: the loved one, the unwanted one, or the hunter?"*

It occurred to him that he might include a score at the end of the "Breakups" section, although he did not really see a reason to assign one. It would not be an easy score to do: in bed, she was a 10. This question had more to do with an overall score, a numerical representation of the satisfaction he had received from that affair. To prevent himself from being overly influenced by the last impressions of their final encounter, which often are terrible, he would assign a score for each section of her file: "Encounter (En)," "Affair (Af)"— that is where the bed comes in— "Breakup (Br)," and then he would average (Av) them to arrive at a final score, which would be penned next to her coded name. For instance, in the case of Rosa Molina López, he would write:

/M1 /L1 / R1 / - / En9 / Af8 / Br5 / - /Av 73% /

Satisfied with his work, he dropped the pen. The advantage of putting things in writing is that it gives you a false sense of reality, especially if the words are capitalized, underlined or enlarged. Graphic magic materializes on the page a referent, which, because it is real, remains unnamable and evasive. There it is, or it seems to be, penned on the paper, a captive butterfly, controlled, and sometimes, dead.

He scrutinized the last thing he had written: Av: 73%. Why didn't I give her a 10? he asked himself. Why, if it's a question of imagination, didn't I give her the coveted 10? This troublesome question drew him to the window. Out of habit, he glanced at the main entrance of his building. He had looked—so many times—from behind the Venetian blinds before answering his intercom that it had become a habit for him to lift the thin sheet of aluminum in order to observe, diagonally, with his left eye, the main entrance to decide whether or not it was convenient for him to answer. Free love brings with it some servitude.

At that moment, it made no sense; no one had called, but Andrés smiled condescendingly, as one who knows himself very well. It was the 10, the beloved ghost had called to him from the vulnerable entrance of desire.

He looked first at the clouds, which, at that moment, darkened the sky above the mountains, and then at the weeds that were invading the street from the open fields three stories below him.

Would he give a 10 to any of his past affairs?

He lay down on the couch with his hands behind his head. When he was young, very young, ecstasy was, logically, his main goal. Every month he fell madly in love with the most beautiful woman in the world. The novelty would wear off after the first stage. All of them are 10's in the beginning. That hope, which Andrés gave up, was the profound impulse of all repetitions, the possibility of resurrecting delirium, the promise of seduction.

The dreamlike enchantment of twilight encouraged him to fantasize. And he suddenly found himself immersed in a childish fantasy, imagining the first woman that would inaugurate the dossier, the first to have her encoded name grace the tab of one of its folders, which vowels would he turn into numbers, what would her measurements be, how he longed to describe her first glance, the first sign of surrender, and, little by little, Andrés was drawn into the rapture of his erotic fantasies, and before he even met that women he was already deeply thankful for her existence. He wondered where she was, how he would meet her, how old she would be, and he continued in this manner until it was time to go out to eat at some place close by, because he did not feel like cooking that night.

## Chapter Three

### *A Blank Page*

It was one of those nights when the moon resembles a slender smile and Venus its lost earring. Elida leaves the movie theater and walks down the avenue. She does not take a bus or a taxi, because she wants to walk, slowly, down the wide sidewalk, without having to avoid people coming in the opposite direction, this way she is simply lost in the cold wind she barely perceives because she is very tired. She crosses the path of two men who are in a hurry, who stare—out of a sense of duty—at her face, then down lower, at her legs, a routine inspection, they would have done the same with any woman, a meaningless gesture because any men + woman + a glance are completely interchangeable for any other men + woman + a glance. Elida knew it, and that is why she ignored them, as she ignored all learned behaviors, so she could walk carefree on a blank page: a page that had started to fade a few months earlier, when she divorced her husband once and for all, when she moved to that crappy apartment with a teeny tiny window up by the ceiling through which, if she stood on a chair, she could see the sunset that was slowly extinguishing itself, when she decided that there would never ever be another man in her life. That page disappeared completely on the same day she invested the last bit of love she had left.

In the customary emptiness that follows divorce, she rescued Amalia from the well of her memories: a mirage, a lifeguard, an intelligent and perverse friend whom everyone had advised her to avoid. And, twenty years ago, they had gone their own ways, despite their friendship. But, when it comes to returning to the past, twenty years is nothing.

She arrived with her small suitcase and her immense enthusiasm, and she asked the doorman for Amalia. In her presence, he pressed Amalia's doorbell and then she heard her friend's voice: Who's there? What's your name? A long silence and then Elida heard: Tell her I don't know any Elida, I'm sorry she must be mistaken. She heard it for herself, the tone of her voice, the solidity of oblivion, so, without persisting, she took her small suitcase, her immense disenchantment and went back to where she had come from.

The white emptiness of her apartment became so apparent that she almost felt like calling her ex-husband to ask him: How are you, are you feeling the same way I am, hoping that he had the same longing for that shared experience of a page that is fading away. But instead she went to the movies, just as she was, in the clothes she had on, exhausted, filthy, in dismay at having had her last connection with the past broken.

And what can Elida do if one day she opens the door of her house to find an abandoned woman curled up in a ball in a basket on the floor? And when she pulls aside the blanket covering the woman, how will she overcome her fear and pity when she discovers that that woman is herself, a barefoot Cinderella without a prince or a fairy godmother to save her?

She thinks that she would like to give herself a new name to create a new character, Wonder Woman, for example, or the intrepid arch-enemy-of-James-Bond chick. But she realized that she could not dream any-more, because reality imposes itself so strongly that it would not allow her to turn things into fiction, and much less believe them. It appears that I've also lost the ability to fantasize, she tells herself out loud. Nothing could heal this loss, she says softly.

She keeps walking through the city, uphill now. It seems to her that pieces are falling from her body, leaving behind a trail of herself, and that the shedding leaves behind her nucleus, a most compact, wordless, nameless, steel core.

Far from downtown, she walks around the luminous traffic circles and arrives at her new neighborhood. Nearby she sees the train pass on the other side of the windbreak of cypress trees. She hears its long whistle, and then a primitive desire to howl springs from her tiny nucleus. She stops, she howls, and she feels great. She smiles. After all, it is possible that that small core contains the best of her essence.

# Chapter Four

## *The Encounter*

Andrés found that night to be exceptionally hot. The tree branches, the entire street, took on the serenity of a movie set. That calm could portend an earthquake or maybe the eminence of a romantic encounter. "The encounter," Andrés murmured to himself, as if he were his own accomplice. A slight euphoria made his body hair stand on end. Somewhere in the city, out there, she is waiting, sitting on a stool in a bar, eating in a Chinese restaurant, or maybe she's alone on a dark street, with a flat tire, and she is looking around in despair, looking for help.

Andrés smiled, surprised by the tenderness that comes over him.

When he entered the bar, he observed the crowd of people for a short while; they were like lively worms in a hole in a tree. He was sure, his intuition more than anything else was telling him, that he would not find her there. Above the sharp shrills of the trumpeter, he saw the same crowd as always. Without fail, as was his custom, his eyes surveyed all the women in his presence. He detected the imaginary lines the men had drawn around the women in the manner of males of all species to protect their territory. He saw the females loitering around the tables, by the bar, sitting, crossing their legs, arching their backs to accentuate their chests, tossing their hair from side to side. He knew most of them, he had had some of them; a few new faces, most of them were being hit on, all of them were beautiful and desirable, that night all of them reminded him of the woman who, somewhere, was waiting just for him, that very special woman worthy of opening the inaugural file of his dossier.

Andrés walked towards the bar feeling he was unique, removed from the assembly-line mentality of erotic consumerism which characterizes nightlife. In response to the bartender's nod, he said: A beer.

That unavailable quality of Andrés's aura captured the attention of two women who sat down next to him. He gave them a quick look over: young, healthy, and available. Condescendingly, as he usually was when approached in this manner, he let them look deeply into his gray eyes; he enjoyed their flirting, their cold calculation, and their physical proximity. He could not help himself, Andrés loved to be seduced. And, by all appearances, that only aroused greater passion in his women. It seemed to awaken a malicious instinct in them that sought to provoke the timid man and pervert the chaste one, something like a challenge to size each other up.

However, that kind of inverse seduction did not appeal to him. He did not have a bad time with those emancipated girls who asked him to go to bed with them at the end of the first date, even though at parties and in bars they revealed the love-making antics of their one-night-stand lovers.

What really turned him on was the challenge, the mystery, the desperate search, the fiery conquest. And, at that moment, he felt that the woman to inaugurate his dossier would have to unleash just such an avalanche of desire and adventure at first glance. And those two chicks did not inspire anything unusual in him; they were just like so many others he had run into.

A feeling of indifference came over him as their pursuit intensified. Andrés was hesitant to open his dossier with just any banal affair. He chose to disengage himself. Andrés's erotic world was put on hold by his desire for a nameless seductress who had already hypnotized him.

For this reason, it did not bother him when a young man with an arrogant countenance succeeded in carrying off the two girls.

He was munching casually on some meat hors d'oeuvres when he heard someone shout his name. From the back of the bar, a group of old friends were calling him to their table. Five men, of every imaginable age and marital status, were planning the night down to the very last detail: liquor, music, pot, porno movies, and—last but not least—the main dish: women.

Andrés enjoyed the rough and tumble camaraderie of this kind of gathering. Nonetheless, after a while he found this habitual misogyny to be strangely suffocating. That kind of humor, which always belittles women, seemed pointless to him. He did not feel comfortable, and with the excuse that a woman was waiting for him—an idea that produced an obscene uproar from his chums—he made his exit from the bar.

If they only knew... He felt pity for himself. The anxiety of his premonition, which almost seemed like a sure thing to him when he left his apartment, had turned into a silly, absurd sensation, especially when he thought about the two girls he had met at the bar. One of them, either of them, could have been the one he was looking for, it was all up to him, or could it be that women are not interchangeable?

He lit a cigarette and, without realizing he was in the middle of the street, started to think things over. Something was happening to him; perhaps forty years had taken a toll on him. He was not looking for a woman; he wanted to fall in love. He had not felt this way in a very long time.

He saw a drunk approaching him, swaggering with the sadness one feels when facing another Monday. He asked Andrés for a cigarette, and went on his way, leaning to one side, as if a great weight in one of his pockets were throwing him off balance.

Andrés sighed out of boredom, with that asthenia that paralyzed him when there was no woman in his life. It has been two weeks since his last "Breakup."

*"It was a bad one, without a doubt. To get rid of her, I had to use the old my-ex-wife-is-coming-back-to-give-our-marriage-one-more-chance story. Even the most persistent women will back away from a returning wife. And if they don't, a couple of children will do the trick. The hard part is convincing them that there really is a wife, because I don't always take the precaution of mentioning "her" every once in a while, just in case. Sometimes I'm afraid that it's a double-edged sword that might inhibit my lover's passion at the moment of her surrender. With this one, I made the mistake of not anticipating a problem. I came to realize that I would need to use this strategy. That girl was stuck to me like glue! She was like a macaw, dying for someone to take care of her so she could abdicate herself from reality. At first, they're all praise, that's for sure, 'Come let me run your life for you...,' but after a while they're worse than a bad case of asthma. If I had to include her in my dossier, the Final Average wouldn't be more than 6."*

The memory of his dossier left Andrés with an intense feeling of emptiness, because there he was, standing in the middle of the night, without anything having happened.

He kept walking, further convinced that he had to find a very special woman—one in charge of herself and her life—win her heart and fall in love with her, in order to experience that vital exaltation, that flood of feelings that Andrés would die for.

When he entered his apartment, the first thing he saw was the practice file he had left on his desk. He missed the company of a pet: a dog, cat, parakeet, turtle, any kind of animal.

Somewhat tired of his solitude, he lay down on his bed with his clothes on. A few seconds later, he heard the doorbell ring. Overcome with joy, he went to the window, lifted the thin sheet of aluminum and peered out. It was a woman. He carefully observed her, but he could not see her clearly. It really did not matter who it was. That night he would gladly accept any unannounced visit. He picked up the intercom phone and answered:

"Hello, who's there?"

"I'm sorry to bother you so late at night," said a timid voice that Andrés could not identify, "I forgot my key and can't get in the front gate. Would you mind opening it for me?"

Andrés did not have to think twice. If he buzzed her in immediately, he would not have a chance to see her. He had to come up with something.

"I would if I could, but my intercom is broken, but I'd be happy to come down to open the door for you. I'll be right there."

He ran to the mirror and, with a quick glance, checked his appearance. He ran a comb through his hair and unbuttoned the top of his shirt, saying: "Oh, Tarzan!" He picked up his keys and rushed downstairs taking three steps at a time.

From the last landing of the staircase, he could see her on the other side of the gate. Andrés did not need to take a second look at her to understand that, despite all his loneliness, she was not the one: she was too small, too insipid; her dress was tacky, her hair was short and too curly. He opened the door with resignation and forced himself to smile in response to her awkward words of appreciation.

He buttoned his shirt and went out to the street for a moment. He contemplated the moon, and then he saw a woman in the distance who was watching the train pass by.

Since Andrés had a childlike faith in the number three, he had a feeling that this third try would do the trick. He approached her slowly, as if he were going to catch a dove. When he was ten yards from her, he stopped in astonishment: she started to howl.

He remembered a piece of advice that a friend had given him a long time ago: Don't get mixed up with a woman who is crazier than you. He talked to himself frequently, especially in the shower or while he was shaving, but he had never, ever—as far as he could remember—howled.

The woman smiled, and then she looked into his eyes as the train disappeared. Andrés was enchanted by her. They looked at each other in silence for a long time. Andrés, having overcome his initial impression, gave her a quick inspection: perfect long, straight hair; tall enough, just right; between twenty-eight and thirty or thirty-two, ideal; nice, long legs, wonderful, and a wide, loose blue blouse prevented her from revealing any more. He was certain that she was the one.

With an exciting sensation of vertigo in his stomach, he approached the woman who had not moved. He was surveying the terrain: upper middle-class, probably educated, she's no novice. He had to be original, creative, and not too obvious.

"I thought that it only happened when there's a full moon."

Perfect, perfect, Andrés said to himself when he saw her smile with amusement. Laughter—a remedy that never fails—weakens all defenses. He waited a while, but she remained silent. Light brown hair, large dark eyes, long eyelashes, a sensuous nose, delicate chin, and full, luscious lips.

Despite her sincere initial smile, her expression was serious. Andrés decided to abandon the humorous approach.

"Do you live around here?" he asked in a casual manner.

"Yes, in an apartment over there," and she pointed with her long, delicate hand towards a gray building at the end of the street.

"Oh, then we're neighbors! I haven't had the pleasure of seeing you before," Andrés said in a tone that became more serious and sugary as he spoke.

He noticed that she turned her glance immediately towards the cypress trees. She's very sensitive; maybe she's reluctant to accept compliments. I'll have to go slower. "It's pleasant to listen to the trains at night," he added, to change the subject.

"Yes, it certainly is," and Andrés saw her lower her eyes.

She's got problems, perfect.

"Please let me walk you home," he said in a courteous manner.

She looked at him attentively. She appeared hesitant. Andrés tilted his head slightly and tried to put on his most innocent smile.

"As you wish," she answered.

She walked in silence, taking long strides. From the corner of his eye, Andrés admired the discreet elegance of her shoes and her gorgeous ankles. She looked magnificent. He was ecstatic about his dossier's first woman. About her file! He had forgotten about the dossier. He needed her first name, last name, marital status. He could not just come out and ask for this information; something told him that he should be cautious, cool, but by now they were within fifty feet of her building. She opened her purse and went through its contents.

"My keys, again," she said in an apologetic tone.

"It helps to always keep them in the same place," Andrés said emphatically.

He said it without thinking, and it worried him. I should have kept my mouth shut; an accusatory tone could scare her away.

"I always misplace my umbrella," he added in commiseration.

"With me, it's sunglasses," she added, nonchalantly, as if nothing had happened. "Here they are," she said with great relief.

Andrés tried to walk more slowly, to delay their arrival, he needed more time. He saw that she had already introduced the key into the lock; he could tell the joke about the drunk who was trying to open his door with the key upside down; he could ask her if she lived with anyone, if he would see her again; he had some tickets, wouldn't she like to go to the theater?

"Well, thank you very much," she said to him as she started to enter the gate. Andrés held the gate with one arm. Time is running out, and he made a move.

"Yesterday was my birthday. I still have a bottle of wine left." I've played my hand, Andrés thought to himself.

"Would you like to have a glass with me?"

Her expression was one of sincere curiosity. Curiosity in a woman is a marvelous thing, Andrés thought, I've found the crack in her defenses.

For a moment she looked away, towards the street, and then she turned towards him with determination and asked him that unexpected question:

"Do you have any glass slippers in size seven?"

"Excuse me?" He wanted more time, he understood nothing, she had thrown him a curve, that woman was a Pandora's Box.

"Nothing, it was just a joke." She smiled, or had she made fun of him? "Forgive me, I just got back from a very... taxing trip." She hesitated in choosing the word taxing. "Maybe another day. Thank you very much."

And she disappeared in the dark hallway, leaving Andrés with the most intolerable frustration he had felt in years.

## Chapter Five

### *The Statistics that Got Away*

All alone, he hit the wall with his fist and returned to his apartment holding in all his rage. Howling, glass slippers, she must be nuts. He paced back and forth in his living room.

The girls at the bar came back to him, "girls, girls, girls," how could I have been so stupid? And he imagined himself with one of the girls, the thinnest one, the one in a white dress, right there in his apartment, in his arms; he saw himself kissing her, removing her tight dress, calculating the size of her waist, her hips, memorizing the shape of her breasts, the color of her nipples, her words, her sighs of pleasure.

He sat down next to the telephone and grabbed his diary. Dozens of numbers, "open files," more than one of them would jump with joy upon hearing his voice, but that crazy woman, that she-wolf, that Cinderella. "What luck!" he murmured to himself, "with so many women in the world, I have to run into this one."

Earlier, on previous occasions, he had thought about this topic. Yes, so many, because in this city and its suburbs there must be 300,000 men and 340,000 women. He questioned the accuracy of these figures, and Andrés, who loves precision for the stability it appears to give in life, got up and took the most recent census report from his bookcase.

He sat down at his desk, put the practice file to one side, and began to write.

*301,270 men*

*333,921 women*

That meant that there were 32, 651 more women than men. Andrés's impatient index finger drummed on the table. There was something fishy about the conclusions he wished to derive from those numbers. Everybody knows that women live longer than men, it's a fact. Of those 333,921 women, how many are old ladies? And how many are little girls?

"I need to know the breakdown by ages," he said out loud, excited about the task he had set for himself. He pulled out his calculator and started to jot down notes. Finally, he wrote:

*Between the ages of 18 and 40, there are: 117,158 men and 131,697 women.*

There were 14,539 more women than men. He confirmed his hypothesis: the difference decreased.

He looked with growing curiosity at the statistics for his county.

| County: | Men: | Women: |
|---|---|---|
| Monte de Oca | 17,223 | 20,252 |

There were 3,029 more women than men. He could not find a breakdown by age, but he calculated that for the age group between 18 and 40, the number would diminish to 1,500 or less. Well, he shrugged his shoulders; a surplus of 1,500 women in just one county is nothing to sneer at.

It would be interesting to know the breakdown by marital status, although to be perfectly honest, when had Andrés ever shown any scruples in his dealings with women that already had partners? *Au contraire*. The sexual paranoia surrounding unsafe sex that seemed to dominate the country in recent years had led him to be more selective.

The possibility of contracting a fatal disease counted—more in theory than in practice—along with his criteria; when it came to an opportunity, he relied more upon a woman's aesthetic appearance and social class than questions of preventative hygiene. He began to prefer fine-looking ladies of a certain age, decent ones or even better yet, married women with their air of unrequited sexual desire.

He returned to the book with increased enthusiasm.

| Population by Marital Status and Gender: | | |
|---|---|---|
| Married: | Men: | Women: |
| Total: | 99,138 | 102,082 |

There are 2,944 absentee husbands! Andrés burst out laughing with the satisfaction of a poacher whose mood had just improved. They couldn't be bigamists, could they?

He checked the numbers for women between the ages of 15 —fifteen, a waste of time!— and 40.

61,714 married women between the ages of 15 and 40.

That's not bad, not bad at all, Andrés smiled. He looked at the next group: divorcees—one of the most interesting to him—known for their insatiable sexual voracity.

| Separated & Divorced | Men: | Women: |
|---|---|---|
| Totals: | 6,049 | 15,837 |

And what does this mean? There are 9,788 surplus women in this group. There are dupes that never learn, and, as soon as they are free —without a woman—they can't hack it, so they are easy prey.

7,231 separated or divorced women between the ages of 15 and 40.

The next figure was for people living together in common-law marriages; what a nice group, Andrés thought to himself, imagining, with duplicitous acceptance, this number doesn't include all the people that belong to this category: love's black sheep.

| Common-Law Marriages | Men: | Women: |
|---|---|---|
| Totals: | 12,759 | 13,271 |

It appeared that in this category, at least in the official reporting, there was agreement between men and women. Nonetheless, Andrés noted the discrepancy in the numbers that suggested the existence of men who take more than their share.

There are 9,766 unmarried women between the ages of 15 and 40 living with their partners.

When he reached the category of widows, Andrés predicted that the number would be disproportionately greater, but, unfortunately, widowhood arrives at a time in life that makes its freedom more pathetic than sexy.

| Status: | Widowers: | Widows: |
|---|---|---|
| Totals: | 2,806 | 14,396 |

There are 787 widows between the ages of 15 and 40.

Just what I thought, Andrés sighed. Beautiful, young, and rich widows have more in common with fairytale characters than real women.

Like many solitary, secretly ambitious men, more than anything else in the world, Andrés would have liked to find a beautiful, rich Jadisha to watch over his dreams, the incomparable mixture of protective mother and consummate lover.

| Single: | Men: | Women: |
| --- | --- | --- |
| Totals: | 106,281 | 116,693 |

There are 72,624 single women between the ages of 15 and 40.

Almost 73,000 single women between the ages of 15 and 40! This figure seemed out of the ball park to Andrés, especially when he imagined all of them together in one place. Unfortunately, these women have to be the most desirable ones for men of any age or marital status. These thoughts made Andrés furrow his brow. He continued to reflect: If we keep in mind that this group includes illiterate women, nuns, lesbians, the infirm, the irremediably hopeless, like the girl that forgot her keys, the howling Cinderella, the picture gets uglier. I wonder if she's single. He picked up the book and with impulsive curiosity searched for the group he found most attractive.

| Professionals, Technicians & Upper-Level Administrators | Men: | Women: |
| --- | --- | --- |
| Totals: | 30,932 | 16,944 |

He could conclude that, in the capital, there were 17,000 professional women, with interesting, good-paying jobs. But he was unable to figure out a way to determine ages or marital status for these 17,000 temptresses.

Having arrived at this impasse, Andrés decided to look out the window. The deserted street reminded him of his unsuccessful attempt at seduction. Somewhat discouraged, he had to admit that his statistical games did not resolve anything, they were of no use. What really counts is something else. And when he said "something else" to himself, he remembered the look on that woman's face as she watched the train disappear. He did not want to think about her. He decided to go to bed.

He took some sleep medication. He had started to undress himself when a memory brought back his lost enthusiasm: "Foreign chicks!" How could he forget them? The beautiful foreign women, the ones that are game for just about anything, the ones that bring so much variety to the monotonous love life of my backwards, gullible village: Caribbean and South-American women, gringas and Canadian women; European, Asian ones, he even had an athletic Australian under his belt, the only woman who had made him feel old at the age of twenty-seven. He picked up the census report with eagerness and wrote:

*Foreign women in San José: 14,609*

*8,200 foreign women between the ages of 15 and 40.*

What a fabulous number! Does this number include female refugees?

He decided not to go there.

His earlier frustration almost forgotten, he could now go to bed more relaxed and satisfied with himself, enveloped by sweet memories of deserted beaches and suntanned female bodies. What would he do on nights like that if it were not for his memories! However, before falling asleep, almost sleepwalking, he headed for his favorite corner of the house where he kept the black briefcase of nostalgia.

# Chapter Six

## *The Power of No*

Elida went up the staircase and stopped in front of apartment number three. She could return quickly to the street, call out to the man and tell him yes, I'll accept your invitation because I don't have anything else to do, or anyone else to talk to. It did not matter that —given this country's crime rate— it was unwise to go to a stranger's apartment for a glass of wine. Had she overlooked common sense, the reasons and purposes of things? Was not life, after all, an empty adventure?

She opened the door and entered her apartment. She felt a smile pulsate throughout her whole body. She watched her small steel core slowly sink in a glass of wine. And then, remembering the disconcerted look on his face when she asked about the glass slippers, she laughed from her heart.

She undressed and got into bed. Something about her attitude towards men had changed. She noticed it that night. The solitude that she had experienced recently had, for the first time, placed her on the same level with men, especially young men. She wondered how old he could be, thirty-two, perhaps thirty-five.

She thought about Federico. Seven years of life together seemed to have magically vanished. Perhaps it is true that only the present exists, this empty present in which to create a new character. But first, Elida had to erase her past, above all that man who had been her whole life. She took photographs, books, gifts, letters, clothing, plants, so that none of her things remained behind, so that the breakup would be real, so that she would not have to imagine that sometime he might look at her picture or remember her body; she wished she could erase herself from his memory! If nothing could be as it was before, then let there be nothing. It was easier that way, or at least she found consolation in the feeling that it was more authentic and more heroic that way. Thinking about it in those terms, she could not help but laugh at herself, at the theatrical bent she had inherited from her mother.

Now she must look to the future; as she said this to herself she thought about the man that had approached her in the middle of the night and the arrogant feeling she had when she turned down his invitation.

Elida refuses to accept that the enthusiasm inherent in a blank sheet of paper—that force which tries to take control of life without regard for others—is real. However, she had felt that sensation when she said no: an extraordinary fullness. It was for her a reencounter with the arrogant little girl that did as she pleased and said no when she felt like it. The impulse of a distant rebelliousness that was lost during her childhood.

She remembered the times when the wind would lift the girls' skirts at the park. The boys would lean to one side to get a better look and then they giggled. Theirs was an incomprehensible laughter, an impregnable fortress that evoked only fear and a defensive response. As well as insatiable curiosity.

Later, when she was a teenager, there were obscene men on the streets, the discussions between boys that she overheard, the ever-present fear of the shame of those that give in to sexual advances, the prestige of saying no, the nuns' warnings, her mother's bitter predictions.

Sex became for her something that men joked about. For Elida, the ideas of sex and being the object of mockery, shame, and ridicule were one and the same thing. Something irrational and painful. Because she sensed with sadness, that for men, and for women too—for almost all humanity—women were those who are inferior, receptive, seducible, gullible, impregnable, and easily deceived.

All of these things, bound to a mythology of consolation built upon a base of relentlessly pure princesses, fairies, sirens, heroes, and princes, contributed to a dream that was both ideal and fatal: a powerful, tender man who would take control over her life, a man as asexual as possible, some kind of intelligent and sensitive eunuch, one capable of overcoming his contradictions and salvaging love.

Elida realized that her dream—as she had dreamt it—would never come true. In spite of much repressed rancor, it was impossible for her to keep masculine desire—that insensible weakness—from overcoming her. A mercenary language kneaded together with rouge, yes, excuse me and thank you very much, she had finally created the necessary structure for submission and distrust. It seemed to her that the meaning of life was to be found outside of herself—in men's lust. She would continue with her rage, the slavery of diets, fashion, and heavy make-up in order to hide her helplessness.

With no other recourse, she became accustomed to walking through that labyrinth, which at times allowed her to get close to paternal and wise figures. And sometimes this approach drew her violently towards the walls of the fortress, where the perverse ones who laugh live, the ones who can—at once—seduce and say no.

Until the day Federico appeared in her life. A university professor, serious, demanding, and—in his own way—kind. From the front row, Elida observed him for four hours each week as he spoke about history, arranged his faded papers and old books, and listened with interest to his students' oral presentations. During an entire year, she cultivated tenderness and admiration for that man who never laughed, for his gray beard, his reputation as a prestigious researcher, and—above all—for his paternal eyes.

He never looked at her with interest, neither at her nor at the other girls. And that was what seemed to confirm for Elida that man's superiority.

She obeyed and loved him in silence. She earned the highest grade in the class and she did not even have the opportunity to say goodbye to him.

Two years later, she ran into him in the archives of the National Library, as solitary as always and lost in his work. But time does not pass in vain. Elida had experienced enough amorous disenchantments with the arrogant inhabitants of the fortress, and she had learned something from them.

The decisive force of nostalgia impelled her to approach him:

"Federico, how are you doing?" and she stretched out her hand without smiling.

"How are you?" he replied to her greeting as he tried to remember who she was.

"You probably don't remember me. I was in your history class two years ago. Elida Arce." She searched in his clear eyes for a flash of recognition. He smiled politely. “Can I talk to you for a moment? It’s about a project I’m working on at the university.”

“I no longer work at the university, I’m retired,” he said, to put an end to the conversation.

“That doesn’t matter. You are still the greatest authority in the field of history.”

In a small cafe in front of the Supreme Court building, Elida told him that she was researching popular legends from colonial times. She told him about a strange belief that existed in a small town in Guanacaste Province. He became very interested in it.

“As summer dragged on and the drought continued to threaten the lives of the people,” she told him, “they looked for an Albino girl to bury a piece of bread in the courtyard of an old house. According to them, that act of magic would make it rain.”

He looked surprised, because he had never heard that legend before. However, it interested him a great deal. Elida insisted that he allow her to consult his large personal library, and he accepted without realizing what she was up to.

The first time that she went to his house, they examined many books together, in monastic silence. She asked to borrow several volumes so she could read— and later discuss— them with him.

The second time, he offered her a cappuccino, and he smiled several times as he talked about the publication he was preparing. She learned that he had been a widower for the past three years and that his children no longer lived with him.

The third time, he was sitting in a dark reclining chair in front of his desk. Thick curtains blocked the clear rays of morning light. Elida passed her fingers over the bookcases; she noticed with interest paintings stained by the humidity, fading diplomas, the stacks of books all over the place, and finally she leaned on the desk, to her left, in front of him.

She observed his gray hair, the tiny lines on the skin of his right check, his delicate lips, the straight hair of his beard, and his eyes which were paler than ever.

They looked at each other in silence. She noticed that his legs were trembling slightly. She watched as his pupils enlarged and his lips parted effortlessly to inquire: "That legend doesn't exist, does it?"

The certainty of having him in her hands, aware of his desire, gave her a sense of power and magnanimity. She felt only gratitude towards him. And in spite of that, she had to tell him.

"No, it doesn't exist."

He lowered his eyes, and Elida, overcome with compassion, finally broke the silence. She moved close to him and sat on his lap. She rested her head on his shoulder and they remained in that position for a long time. His eyes were closed and the trembling of his legs had become uncontrollable. He slowly leaned his head towards her, until his lips were close to hers, which opened to kiss him. Their first contact confirmed the sweet fire that came over them, the incredible harmony of their intertwined tongues.

Elida felt him run his fingers through her hair, rub her temples, caress her cheeks and shoulders, traverse her waist and grab hold of her legs in order to press her firmly to his groin. She heard her name moaned for the first time, and the trembling of his legs spread in a convulsion throughout his body.

Elida embraced him with increasing force to protect that torrent which, by now, was beyond control.

From that day forward, the armchair became the exclusive setting for their love. In response to Elida, who would have preferred to visit the city's more unusual places, Federico was always hermetically negative.

Sitting together on the couch, strolling through his small garden or drinking coffee on the front porch, they would enthusiastically discuss any topic. Without touching each other. Elida was intrigued by the astonishing things that Federico knew.

One of them, usually her, looked for a way to end up in that dark reclining chair where they always remained quiet, without looking into each other's eyes, where she always sat on his lap so that he could hug and kiss her, caress her body with his strong hands, hands that rubbed—with insistence and desperation—circles inside the ultimate object of his desire.

Elida already loved him with an unconditional affection, when, without warning, he surprised her one afternoon with the unexpected violence of his desire, when he stopped cradling her in his arms in order to devastate her body without tenderness.

They remained on the carpet in silence, without looking at each other. Elida thought she noticed a small spot on one of her eyes that projected a grayish shadow upon any object she looked at.

She told herself—as if she had known and accepted it all along—that she could not expect Federico to break the mold of his gender: he was a man.

They did not see or talk to each other for several days. Emptiness and nostalgia began to occupy her solitary afternoons. One Sunday morning, Elida received a large bouquet of lily of the Nile flowers. The card just said: "Don't abandon me, I need you." Elida took his request so seriously that she married him some time later.

# Chapter Seven

## *The Great Dane*

Andrés arrived punctually at the laboratory and greeted his fellow workers. The walls, floor, and long counters covered with white Formica reeked of disinfectant. In a voluntary attempt to get into his routine, he straightened bottles, test tubes, agents, forms, and he was transported to another place—without intending it—absorbed in a leafless oak tree under a lead-colored sky.

A routine job, without any responsibilities, offers great advantages for a dreamer like Andrés. He remembered with some annoyance his insipid weekend and—with contradictory and mixed feelings—the strange woman who had howled at the passing train.

A firm slap on his back from a fellow worker distracted him from his thoughts.

"What's up, Andrés? How was your weekend?" He asked, winking at him.

"Fine, just fine. Nothing out of the ordinary," he replied, thinking about the inflated expectations people harbor.

"Have you seen the Great Dane?"

"No, I haven't seen anyone. What's this about the Great Dane?"

"Don't you remember they were going to send an inspector to scrutinize our control systems? Well, they sent a woman inspector. And what a woman she is!" he added as he traced opulent curves with his hands in the air. "That Dr. Halstt is built like a brick shit house!" Andrés smiled as he remembered the category of foreign women in his nocturnal statistics. He started to work as his colleague continued to talk about the woman inspector who had just arrived. All the myths seemed to fit like a glove: She was a blond, very tall and beautiful foreigner; she was rich and open minded; she had a doctorate. She was technologically savvy, she was a representative of investors that dealt in U.S. dollars, and she had the power to produce a report capable of sinking all of us.

"What's her name?"

"Ingrid Halstt. It's a pretty name, don't you think? And she's involved with the big boss..."

Andrés did not have to look for news regarding women; it came looking for him. He was obligated by his friends to hear any and all of that kind of gossip. In spite of his prudence and his principle of not bragging too much about his conquests, they considered him the prototype of the die-hard seducer, especially the married ones who openly envied his bachelorhood, the ones who filled in the details that Andrés left out with their wild fantasies.

During his coffee break, Andrés went to a café and sat at the table next to his regular buddies, an exclusive group of men who frequently laughed and talked boisterously. One of them nudged his elbow.

"Andrés, there's the Danish woman."

Andrés turned around and looked with interest at the extremely tall blond with enormous breasts who entered accompanied by the boss. Without setting it as goal for himself, he thought it would be interesting to make love to such a tall woman.

When he left, Andrés passed by the group which included the doctor. His gaze crossed that woman's clear blue eyes. With feigned respect, he approached her and extended his hand towards her.

*"God Dag,* Dr. Halstt."

She smiled with pleasant surprise and squeezed Andrés's hand with Nordic firmness.

*"God Dag,"* she responded.

Andrés noticed with amusement the surprise of his fellow workers and the obvious discomfort of his boss.

Back at work, with laughter and slaps on his back, they drilled him with questions.

"I had a Danish girlfriend a long time ago," he told them as if it were no big deal.

Lost in meticulous tasks, Andrés allowed himself to be carried away by the peace found in routine. Reality became a piece of cake for him in those moments when everything was predictable and when there was no anxiety.

He smiled to himself, remembering his boss's expression. Andrés would not try to get even with his boss that way. He had always tried to keep his very special personal life—women—separate from his work. Moving between those two opposite and complementary worlds enriched both of them, making for a more amenable existence.

The few affairs that had presented themselves at the workplace had taken on a weird domestic complexion, which had made him lose interest almost immediately. For Andrés, such closeness to reality made it difficult to keep the magic alive. Only one woman had made him disregard that principle in the past three years he had worked at that business: an exotic director of human resources, with ivory skin and incredible eyes, with whom he had maintained a dangerous relationship in dark corners and hiding places throughout two torrid months.

Now it was the Danish woman. He enjoyed himself imagining the prestige that that conquest would give him in the eyes of his fellow workers. But he did not want to run the risk or awaken jealousy in his boss who could surprise him with a pink slip at any moment.

On the other hand, he did not have to pad his reputation. It was already set in stone.

# Chapter Eight

## *Rendezvous at Ten*

He sat down at an impeccably clean counter. He examined the neat row of samples that he was to analyze. A sudden indifference came over him. He remembered—like a thorn in his finger—the woman from the apartments. Where did he go wrong? Maybe he invited her to his house too soon, or perhaps the comment about the key distanced her from him, or maybe he didn't compliment her enough, or maybe he was too shy. She might be one of those women who call for the direct, straightforward approach: you put your arm around her waist, so that she can feel, with the right contact, your hand, your body, so that she fears, she gets the picture, whisper something into her ear at the right moment, just as she's leaving, a drop of burning poison that will begin to ferment in her imagination until it matures into the urgent desire to live out her fantasies.

How he longed to see that howling Cinderella dying for him, begging him, calling him on the phone, sending him love notes, chasing him in the bars, in the streets, after work; that fatiguing and pathetic pursuit, which is tiring in most cases, especially when it follows what appeared to be a good and final breakup; he longed for her now with desire and revenge, to see her in complete surrender and to drag things out, provoke desperation, crying, and finally to give in to the most sweet amorous frenzy.

Through experience, Andrés had reached the conclusion that one of the most effective ways to drive a woman crazy was to introduce—at the most opportune moment—a game of ambiguities within the regular routine. To be arbitrary without exaggerating; to be somewhat cruel, committing injustices for no reason at all.

When he did this, Andrés behaved toward women like that long-tailed animal with a kangaroo face dreamt by Kafka. When he would try to grab the animal's tail, the animal would pull it out of the way, and

Kafka became relaxed until the tail caught his attention again, and, when he tried to trap it again, the animal would pull it away again. Kafka had the impression that that animal was trying to train him.

Andrés set about to initiate this game as quickly as possible: a week, a day after meeting her, at the first chance that circumstances would allow. As soon as an attraction was confirmed through unmistakable glances, telephone calls, false fortuitous encounters, invitations, small gifts, caresses or tender goodbye kisses, Andrés would pull his tail away at the slightest attempt to possess him. In this way, he provoked that kind of tension, uncertainty, and curiosity that reconfirmed and intensified their interest in him.

Almost without exception, they would go into a hypnotic state, repeating over and over again the game of trying to catch his tail every time he would let them see it. In this way, he drove them mad with desire to possess him completely, just as he had planned.

But what would work with that woman, how could he awaken her interest? This uncertainty haunted him all day long. He tried to put it out of his mind, to ignore it, to deny its existence, but this only served to drive the thorn deeper and deeper into his flesh. The more absurd the idea became, the more inevitable it was.

When he got home, after drinking two shots of vodka in a bar, he stopped to observe the gray apartment building. He counted the floors and windows. He deduced that there were six apartments on each floor. He walked right up to the door that she had entered and saw six intercom buttons. He pressed them one by one asking the same question:

"Does the woman interested in the glass slippers live here?"

No one was interested, and number three was the only one that did not answer.

Andrés concluded that she lived there, in number three. This symbolic concession that fate had presented to him was a confirmation that he had made the right decision. He went home prepared to make official something that was already inevitable: the first file of his dossier.

| / / / En.10 / Af. / Br. / Av. | |
|---|---|
| 1. General Information: | |
| Age: 28 -32?<br>Race: White<br>Virginity: Unlikely?<br>Zodiac Sign: ?<br>Hair: light brown, straight, shoulder-length<br>Eyes: large and dark<br>Lips: voluptuous<br>Weight: 130 lbs.?<br>Height: 5'5"?<br>Waist: ?<br>Breasts: ?<br>Hips: ?<br>Birthmarks: ?<br>Other details: ? | Nationality: Costa Rican<br>Marital Status: ?<br>Children: ?<br>Religion: ?<br>Contraceptive Method of Choice:?<br>Profession: ?<br>Place of Employment: ?<br>Income: High?<br>Address: 75 La Rotonda Mini Market<br>Telephone: ?<br>Car: Probably not?<br>Tobacco, Liquor, Drugs: No?<br>Hobbies: ?<br>Shared Acquaintances: ? |

| DRAWING: | |
|---|---|
| Frontal View: | Rear View: |

| 2. Personal Information: |
|---|
| Laconic, quiet. Intense, nostalgic look in her eyes. Worried smile. Smooth, relaxed stride. Unsettling behavior. Mysterious. Elusive. Conservatively dressed, shoes and clothes of high quality. Little makeup. A soft, somewhat low voice. |
| 3. Development: |

4. Encounter:

I met her on Sunday, September 4, 1988, in front of my house. It was around midnight. She was alone, standing there in the middle of the street watching the train pass by. When I was a few steps away from her, she started to howl. The train whistle blew in the distance while she was looking at me. Her appearance and strange reaction led me to choose the humorous approach. It worked at first, because she laughed and even allowed me to walk to her home, just twenty-five yards from my own apartment. I think she lives in apartment number three. Because time was running out, I invited her right then to share a glass of wine with me in my apartment. She turned down my offer. Instead, she asked me a strange question: if I had any sparkling glass slippers in size seven. I suppose it was an allusion to Cinderella, although it was probably more a rhetorical question than anything else. I don't think a mature woman—one who as far as I can tell is well off—goes around searching for a prince. However, she did mention a difficult journey, and something in her attitude and expression gave me the impression that she has a problem. But it would have been precipitous of me to try to discover something about her then or to try to take advantage of her in her first moment of vulnerability. On the other hand, that woman exudes a powerful, magnetic halo that invades your senses.

I think I made two mistakes. I should have used a more direct approach, complimenting her beautiful eyes or something like that and making it clear to her that I was interested in her as a woman. I also messed up by not arranging a date for our next meeting. She told me—and these are her words— "Some other time." I should have insisted right then, when? I'll be counting the days, or any other display of an instant crush. Another big mistake was not having asked her name, not introducing myself. Judging by her appearance, I would say that she likes to keep things formal. I haven't been able to forget the first time she looked at me. Her intense eyes landed on mine like the Phoenix in flames. That unforgettable fire is what convinced me to give her a 10 in this section of her file, even though at first glance it looks like I failed. I don't want to bet on it, but I'm not giving up.

## Chapter Nine

### *Nostalgia for Paradise*

Tuesday morning. Andrés left his house and, instead of going to the bus stop, he turned right. He had not intended to do so, but he headed straight towards the gray apartment building.

That morning was extremely clear, and the cypress trees of the windbreak swayed in the breeze. He had a wonderful feeling of adventure, and without realizing it, he walked along like a brave hunter in the middle of a jungle.

He stopped in front of the gate and rang number three. Each second that passed with no reply darkened his morning. He called again, and the obstinate silence returned to him the status of an ordinary man who sets off every morning for work, and nothing more.

He does not like—it displeases him—to feel this way; an anarchic part of him is out of his control. He realizes that it has to do with that woman, and that makes him furious.

Waiting for the bus, he shares—although he would prefer not to—the lethargic routine air of that row of salaried employees, housewives, school children, and one or another individual who does not fall into any category, like the guy in the white suit with the ruddy face and Lincolnesque beard. Andrés has never grown a beard, just a thick black mustache that goes with being Costa Rican.

He stops thinking as the centipede-like line of people gets on the bus. Fortunately, he is able to secure a seat, which spares him the thirty-five minutes of being tossed around like a leaf had he not gotten one.

A young woman wearing a miniskirt—the first thing he notices—sits down next to him. She had the kind of long fingernails that he would expect to find behind a slow window in a government office. Then there was her transparent blouse that made him think, a cute tiny blouse, he says it is cute because the slightest flirtatious gesture in a woman makes him feel thankful to her, as if that gesture, every gesture, were directed specifically at him, and he was thankful to her, because Andrés felt that any innocent gesture in a woman was directed at him.

He observes with pleasure the angle of the lower part of her breasts and the profile of the young woman's button nose. Andrés perceives—or believes he perceives—the girl looking at him from the corner of her eye.

He takes a deep breath. He feels a little better, relaxed, beside that young woman who is becoming, through Andrés's innate power of synthesis and generalization, the WOMAN, who fulfills her role—in the way in which that morning he needed, dreamt, and desired that women would.

"Where are you getting off?" he asked her with confidence.

"Excuse me?" she answered, batting her eyelashes to Andrés's delight.

"I said where are you getting off?"

"Oh, at the courthouse."

"Is that where you work?"

"Yes, in the Patent Office."

"How interesting!" he smiled, thinking how appropriate. "Do you always catch the bus here? ... I've never seen you before," he said with emphasis.

Andrés noticed a smile of contentment; this is good, he thought.

"That's because I have to go in early, we have a training seminar."

"Oh, how wonderful! When do you get out?"

"At five," and she began to stutter.

"I get out at five too. How about if I wait for you after work?" he asked nonchalantly.

"Oh no, I can't."

Who is she kidding, and what about the way she looked at me? He tried to hide his annoyance.

"Why?"

"I have a boyfriend; he always walks me home. He works at the same place," she added.

He always walks her home, how clever, he said to himself looking towards the street. She was serious the rest of the trip and they did not say anything else.

When she stood up to get off, Andrés checked out her profile—this time with annoyance—because that blouse and miniskirt were slipping through his fingers.

And with the same feeling of annoyance, he got off the bus and headed towards the factory where he worked. As he walked, he thought about women and his dossier. That business had become an unnecessary burden that he had created for himself just for the hell of it.

Once he was in his laboratory, he put on a white coat and thought about how he would prefer to skip all that seduction stuff, so that things would happen just like in his erotic fantasies and sometimes in real life, with no need for seduction or tedious preludes, without the risk of rejection, insatiable women that offer themselves, give themselves, beyond one's efforts, merits or what one has earned, outside the market of supply and demand, a paradise.

It was a terrible and eternal Tuesday. The bacteria count for one of their products was extremely high and his boss, who was great at delegating his own work, assigned Andrés the task of complaining to the people at the plant. Anger relieved the tension he felt inside, and he kept practicing this technique with his co-workers in the lab, in the cafeteria, with secretaries, and, in his imagination, with the Great Dane who was never around. He smoked a pack-and-a-half of cigarettes and got a horrible migraine headache.

For this reason, when he left work he allowed himself the luxury of waving down a taxi. He could not wait to get home to drink that bottle of wine; why should he wait, for whom? He could go by Yoyo's house for some pot; no way, after all, it would be nicer to drink some wine, put on some music, and sleep. He would play some tango music, the music he always listened to when his morale was low, "one drags oneself through thorns and in his desire to give his love..." Damn women, he muttered to himself with rage, I'm forty and I'm still playing this game; maybe I should settle down and get married. The figure of his mother repeating those words came to pull him from the abyss into which—with the taxi's vibrations and memories of tango music—he was falling.

He looked out the window and noticed that it had started to get dark. Light rain covered the windows with tiny beads of water. "Right here, on the right side, the yellow house. How much do I owe you?"

"Three fifty."

Before he could complain about the price—What does the meter say? —he saw the woman briskly passing by along the sidewalk.

"Here!"

The taxi driver turned his head around looking for the money. Andrés hurriedly pulled out and dropped some money on the front passenger seat and took off after his neighbor without waiting for his change.

When he reached the gate, she was already gone. He heard her heels climbing the staircase.

"Hey, wait a minute!" he shouted.

The sound of her heels stopped for a second.

"I'm the guy from the other night, can we talk?"

He heard her heel on the staircase again and then saw her face peeping over the stair rail. Her silky hair hanging down. Her eyes were on him attentively.

Andrés, from behind the bars of the front gate, asked:

"What's your name?"

"Elida."

Andrés could not think of anything else to say, and Elida disappeared again. He had choked, he was unable to react.

It started to rain very hard, and Andrés finally allowed himself to smile.

What the hell! ... a blow below the belt. How can her name be Elida? How can you seduce a woman who has the same name as your mother?

He racked his memory trying to remember some other Elida in his past, but he could not remember a single one. Out of curiosity he went through the names of his friends' wives, fiancées, girlfriends, and lovers. Not one of them had his mother's name, but there must be a lot of Elidas around. Lost in his labyrinth of thoughts, he did not hear Elida's voice. He felt someone tapping him on the shoulder.

"And you, what's your name?" she asked him from the other side of the gate.

"Andrés" he answered her with eagerness, by now recovered from his surprise. "I saved a bottle of wine just for you," he added not wasting any time.

"Red or white?"

"Red."

"Then you can keep it for a long time."

"Is it going to take that long for you to accept my invitation?"

Andrés contemplated her smile with excitement: she's on the verge of accepting. In that instant, he wished he had the magic formula to make her fall into his arms, a love potion, hypnotism, a prayer from a blessed soul, the shortcut to reach the happy ending of his fulfilled desires.

"It could be tomorrow, if that's okay with you," she said with hesitation.

"What about today, right now, or if you prefer, in an hour?"

"Fine, Andrés, let's make it an hour from now. See you then."

"I'm in apartment number seven, don't forget!"

He smiled, his eyes were glowing, she said my name, recalling the proof of his success, an omen of the fantastic evening ahead of him. He started to feel alive again. On the way to his apartment he picked the three freshest red hibiscus flowers in the garden at the entrance to his building. Flowers were an essential part of his routine.

He placed them carefully in a ceramic vase. The round vase in his hands reminded him of Cristina, one of the youngest, sweetest women he had ever had. It was a gift from her for the flowers she brought him every time they had a date.

He set the hibiscus flower arrangement at the center of the wicker coffee table and he relived her childlike hands that he taught how to caress. A wonderful memory, Cristina, made possible because she left before their desire died. The second "nice" girl whose parents had sent her out of the country to keep her away from Andrés. Everybody called Andrés "Passport Brenes" in those days, and Andrés boasted about his nickname, enjoying the areola of lady-killer he had acquired.

Next to the flowers he lit an incense stick, and beside it were the bottle of wine and two wine glasses.

He checked his apartment carefully. In the bedroom, he chose to leave the comforter on his bed; he spread it out neatly. He arranged the white llama rug at the foot of the bed. He selected a yellow towel from his closet and hung it on the towel rack in the bathroom next to his own. He rearranged the shower curtain and then stopped in front of the mirror. He did not need a shave. He stared at himself trying to guess how she would see him. In his eyes, he observed an unexpected arousal overcoming him as he imagined the look of desire in her eyes. He smiled thinking: an excellent sign.

He searched for his "inventory" of prophylactics and tucked two in the back pocket of his pants. On previous occasions, women had told him "You're using a rubber or you ain't getting any." He had come to accept as an article of faith that using a condom while making love was like taking a shower with a raincoat on or, even better, like eating a piece a candy with its wrapper on. It was the spirit of the age, and Andrés had completely adopted the idea.

On the other hand, it was not a big deal for him. Even as a young man, he had become an expert. No one could match his speed and expertise. He could put it on, at any time and in the most awkward of positions, with one hand—without a woman noticing the slightest interruption in their foreplay.

He was planning his moves when the phone rang. A velvety-soft voice on the other end.

"Hello sweetheart, how are you?"

He did not recognize her voice at first, but he went along with her.

"Well, hi, fine."

"That's all you have to say to me, che? It only took you two years to forget about me?"

"How can you think that?" That word che, meaning "guy" in Argentina and Uruguay, gave her away. "Vicky, you are an incredible woman.

When did you arrive?"

"This afternoon. I'm going to be in town a few days. Will you invite me out for a drink?"

"What kind of question is that, Vicky? A thousand drinks, anything you want." Andrés's mind raced, this week is already booked in case I get lucky with my neighbor. "I'm really busy these days, what about next Monday at seven?"

"That's groovy, sweetheart! If you're free any earlier, I'm at Grace's pad."

"Ciao, baby."

Andrés hung up the phone. He was flying, elated, feeling young, sought after, powerful, just like when he was in his prime, when women would line up in a spiral shaped circle around him, so that, when one of them was in the center of romance, the others whirled around that privileged space, seduction and breakups were simultaneous, with Andrés—like an octopus—in control of everything.

# Chapter Ten

## *The Strategy of Weakness*

He sat down on the couch and lit up a cigarette. He looked at his watch: he still had twenty-five minutes to wait. It did not matter, he could wait. He was at peace with time.

He got up and put on a CD of romantic ballads by the Brazilian singer Roberto Carlos, almost every woman loves his songs. Seven o'clock rolled around, then seven-thirty, and then eight o'clock. The CD had just finished playing "Suddenly, there was love..." When?

Andrés paced from one side to another, nervously, fearing the wrath that would overcome him if that woman did not show up; he was already planning what to do: give someone a call, go out for a few drinks. The last thing he would think of doing would be to go to her apartment; one should never forget the power relationship that underlies love; one should not reveal his weaknesses unless it is part of a strategy. He smoked and smoked and smoked, and then suddenly the doorbell rang. It was a quarter past eight, but that doesn't matter as long as she is here now.

Andrés forgot everything when he saw her entering his house: in very tall high heels, her long legs, soft hips, gardenia perfume, the way she moved herself, her smile, her silky hair, everything else was forgotten. Like a fisherman who casts his line from the side of his boat knowing that this is the time—that beneath the waves a great catch awaits him—Andrés was certain that finally Elida would be his.

That is why, when she got up, looked at her watch, and said: "I've got to go," Andrés went crazy.

Elida had entered his apartment with a sense of measured ease. She praised the way the apartment looked and how neat everything was, and she smiled to herself when she saw the enormous metal file cabinet occupying a privileged place in the living room. She looked at Andrés with a disconcerting sincerity: nothing in her comportment could be construed as seductive or coquettish. She sat down in an armchair and crossed her legs. They toasted to each other's health. Elida started to talk and Andrés started storing information for his first file. As she spoke of her life, Andrés was busy making plans. He discovered that she had been divorced for a few months, she had no children, lived alone, and did not have a telephone. She possessed a master's degree in social work, and she held a sterile bureaucratic job she wanted to quit in an institution for alcoholics. It was as if she were starting all over again at this point in her life. An auspicious opportunity for Andrés, but a dangerous one.

Andrés asked her questions, acted interested in everything she said, tried to make intelligent observations, and feigned absolute attention while at the same time he pondered over her possible weaknesses. By the way she crossed her legs and lifted her knees, he deduced that that was where he should begin. If she displays them in that manner, she must be proud of them. And Andrés always started with each woman's favorite part of her own body. It was reassuring to them, it affirmed for them their charms, something that made things easier for him.

As she talked about her divorced parents, her lonely childhood, he was waiting for the right moment to sit down beside her, to look into her eyes and gently place his hand on her knee. He would tell her this had never happened to him before, that he had never met a woman who he could not stop thinking about.

He decided that the best thing to do was to act like a victim of Cupid's sweet and painful arrow as his hand migrated up her skirt to a prudent point to allow him to evaluate her reaction. Then he would try to kiss her red lips that moved seductively as she spoke.

When she told him how her father had left the house with a younger woman, Andrés imagined himself caressing her exquisite legs. If she were to close her eyes, sigh or smile: perfect, full speed ahead.

If, on the contrary, she were to impede his advance, he was planning to adopt —egregiously wounded—a strategy of tactical retreat. He would persist—with feigned resignation—in his role as victim: a lonely guy who falls hopelessly in love with a woman who rejects him.

Right from the start he took the time to give her clues, the necessary information, so she would understand him: a sensitive and lonely man, with a lot of experience in life, with no permanent attachments to anyone, stalked—that is the right word for it—by many women that he—unfortunately—found to be too empty, too young, and too immature.

Andrés used this line with women over thirty, the dominant and protective and not-too-beautiful type. It had a double purpose: on one hand, it made them feel that their age was an advantage; on the other hand, it made it clear to them that he was an expert who was not blown away by frivolous beauty queens—a deep man, available for a serious monogamous relationship, in need of the understanding and love of a special woman. Even a little love would make him happy.

Andrés had heard it said that women love men more for what they themselves can do for their men than for what their men can do for them. With women like Elida, charitably inclined ones, it was generally successful. It could not fail.

He observed her long, delicate fingers, which she moved expressively as she talked about the money her father used to send her to pay tuition at a preparatory school and then at the university, and Andrés could picture those hands running through his hair as he kissed her with wild abandon.

They would do "it" right there, in that same armchair; it was comfortable, and there was no reason to disrupt anything by going somewhere else. Fortunately, she was wearing a skirt and nylons. His mind was on these things when he saw her get up, look at her watch, and say: "I have to go." It was then that Andrés lost control of himself.

"But you just got here, Elida. Please don't do this to me. Since I met you I have been dreaming about this moment. Please don't go."

He approached her and put his arms around her, trying to find her lips to kiss her. Elida reacted immediately, moving her face away from him, she pushed him with her fists, repeating: "Are you nuts, leave me alone, I don't want to do that," while Andrés was pushing her against the wall, pursuing her neck, her waist, he squeezed her legs, "I'm crazy about you," he told her, "since the first time I saw you, I've dreamed of this moment," murmurs, shouts, hugs, kicks, two bodies wrestling one another, agitated, panting, on the verge of the most exhilarating violence.

Andrés, in his impetuous haste, knocked Elida onto the couch. She tried to get up but could not move because Andrés's strong body was on top of her.

Andrés pulled down his pants. He started to unbutton his shirt but then decided that that was not essential. There are a few, crucial moments when it is impossible to dress in one's birthday suit—like Adam in all his perfect splendor and glory—so you just do it the way you are. So, he went straight for Elida's skirt. He had already reached her waist when the feel of the soft and warm skin of her belly increased his passion to an unbearable degree. Elida recognized the weakness in his sighs, your skin, he had said, and, in one final effort, she spun around and, with all her might, threw him off the couch.

The small wicker coffee table fell over. The ashtray, the breaking of glass, flowers and the silver incense holder rolled across the floor. From there, Andrés's surprised and desolate eyes watched her as she got up and straightened her clothes.

Andrés picked himself off the floor slowly, moving like a sleepwalker who has just been awakened. All of a sudden, he felt exhausted from the struggle, worn out by his long, frustrating expectation, spurned, depressed, fed up and, above all, sad, because at that moment he wanted her more than ever.

Elida observed him with seriousness in her eyes. She was also confused, not knowing what to do or feel about that unexpected calm, following—with distress and anxiety—the deliberation of Andrés's movements as he started to take off all his clothes until he was completely naked in front of her.

She watched him lie down on the couch. After staring at her for a long time in silence, he closed his eyes and remained completely still. Elida approached him with curious fascination.

Just like the wolf lies down on the ground to offer his helpless neck to his aggressor, Andrés abandoned himself to secure final victory in his battle. Because, when Elida saw him in that position, in a position of trusting surrender that she could never imagine in any man, she felt a deep tenderness. She leaned over his strong, dark body and caressed him without pausing, generously, until she made him completely happy.

## Chapter Eleven

### *Unknown Tyrant*

Elida lay down on her bed without undressing, with the lights off, and did nothing. She could not, she did not want to take her mind off the image that had taken control of her fantasy: that naked man offering himself to her. Over and over again, she relived what she had felt at that moment—surprise, delight, even her eyes were captivated by his spell; an immobilized man, a statue just for her, a present, she the protagonist, the possessor, the dominant one, the absolute owner of his desire, contemplating his sweet face lost in pleasure, pleasure that she was giving him like a magician, a goddess, owner of his soul, bringing him back to life.

She did not want him to look at her afterwards, she did not want questions, she did not want to analyze their disconcerting situation. Without saying a word, she left, knowing that her footsteps were wandering in a different dimension, oblique, distant, an arrow returning to the origin of desire where a small girl contemplates with fear the strong fortress of the warriors.

She got up as if she was awakening from an unresolved, enigmatic dream, and she went to make some tea for herself. The usual noises of doors and dishes, the tea's aroma, sugar, teaspoon, reached her from afar, an exigency, the rational mind searching for meaning, searching for the next step. And Elida smiled when she formulated the disturbing and amusing question that she was facing: If I wanted to get rid of Cinderella and, once and for all, dispense with the unlikely prince, what role could this man have in my life, this Sleeping-Beauty type?

She went back to bed and, with small sips, drank her tea. It took her a long time to fall asleep because she refused to stop recreating that event in its most minute details.

Finally, sleep arrived to complete its work of processing the day's events. That unknown tyrant, who rules the underground world, forges and shapes events with the hidden desires and fears of each individual's personal history. The mysterious, camouflage version abandons the rest of the experience like the June bug sheds its shell.

That was what Elida found when she woke up: the disconcerting memory of meaningless events, as if a stranger had just revealed them to her. She refused to believe them; she closed her eyes tightly to keep them away, to negate them.

But there they were, undoubtedly they were real, as real as the things she had felt then which now seemed alien to her. The more she thought about that night, the more she regretted everything: accepting his invitation, allowing his advances, finally giving in to his pleading desire, succumbing and losing once again.

The memory that pained her the most was having pretended that she could talk seriously about her life to him; she even imagined that that man, who seemed to listen and to understand her, could become her confident, a friend with whom she could talk and share her life, a source of support to help her keep going in life.

Her longing for him to come to her, to sit down by her side, embracing her with tenderness, now seemed ridiculous to her. She thought that if he did that, and if he were also to softly caress her hair, she could cry, almost with joy, all the tears that she had swallowed during the past several months.

It seemed ridiculous because he was not interested in her life, neither in the emptiness of her life nor the fear she felt in confronting her solitude alone. The reality that Elida had been putting off for as long as she could remember.

It was a fact that none of this was of any interest to him. She remembered the grief that rose to her lips, inaudible to her at that moment, when she discovered in his eyes the look of a lascivious animal: It was not what she longed for, the same thing again.

She remembered everything now, and she revived—relived—the disgust that shook her whole being to the core when she encountered the ravenous stickiness of that man, her anger at his violence, his invincible physical power. And then, the same old trap, the impossibility of abandoning him, to say no. Why didn't I leave? Elida tortured herself over and over again.

## Chapter Twelve

### *The Naked Female Soul*

Andrés remained on the couch for a long time, disturbed, mulling over in his mind the scene that had taken place a few moments earlier. He relived his struggle with Elida's body, a struggle that even surprised him. He saw himself taking his clothes off, observed by Elida with the eyes of one who watches a magician on a stage. And then, those timid, awkward hands that approached to caress him with a determination as unexpected as the pleasure they brought him.

Curiously, he felt neither euphoric nor triumphant. That sense of unreality was alien to him. He remained in the shower for a long time, enjoying the flow of water on his empty head.

He slowly got dressed and then sat down at his desk. He opened the metal file cabinet and contemplated the empty spaces between the hanging folders for a long while. Elida Arce Abarca. He had not foreseen that the initial letters of a woman's name could be a vowel, just as he had not anticipated that his dossier's first entry would have the same name as his mother. Far too many unforeseeable things had transpired, and this, far from motivating him, was for Andrés a matter for concern. He looked up the numerical code for vowels and he wrote:

/ 3R / 3B / 7L /

Three and seven, he uttered, accepting once again the coincidences. He reviewed the list of General Information, filling in the missing items.

Thirty-three years old, one more than I thought; Costa Rican, divorced, no children, Virginity—no way, Contraceptive Method of Choice—not a clue; Zodiac Sign—no idea, although she must be a Cancer; Religion—no way of knowing; College Education, Social Worker at the Institute for Alcoholics, average income—but I'm not sure; I'd better wait until I learn more about her; will we see each other again? No phone, no car, she doesn't smoke, she drank little, she didn't seem as tall as the other night, she's probably only 5'4".

When he reached the categories of Waist, Chest, and Hips, he remembered surrounding Elida's tense body with his arms, her voluptuous thighs, the warm skin of her belly, and he felt something in his chest becoming warm and liquid. At the same time, a great barrier arose between him and his dossier. As if it were an unavoidable and shameful duty, he tried to think about her measurements as a carpenter would if he were measuring a piece of furniture. He concentrated on the size of her breasts.

He had always liked women with medium-sized, firm, well-rounded breasts. Experience had taught him that women with small breasts tend to be more intelligent and are more forward. However, they are almost always less affectionate and more reluctant to surrender themselves at the moment of truth. Moderation here, as in all things, is the best policy. And, as far as Andrés could discern, Elida fell into that felicitous category. She's probably a size 36C. The Venus de Milo is a 38, and most of the gringo girls I've met have been 39's. He smiled, his best memories having brought back his fine sense of humor. So he wrote down the following: approximately 36 inches.

His memory traveled to her tiny, delicate waist. He tried to imagine her naked. He could see her long torso, forming a smooth curve, a flat stomach, and a firm belly: the smooth, well-defined body of a woman who has not been pregnant, the strange and fascinating body of a mature adolescent. As if awakening from a delightful dream, he focused once again on her figure: Waist, around 24 inches. Hips, about 38 inches.

He looked at the next category: DRAWING. On a separate sheet of paper, he started to scrawl Elida's body as he had imagined it. He tried to sketch her face, her hair; he attempted to draw her waist and hips. It was impossible to capture the life and beauty of that body. He felt absurd. He scratched out the word DRAWING and went to the next section: 3. DEVELOPMENT.

## B. AFFAIR:

I don't know what happened. I had a strange and violent reaction when she said she was leaving. I couldn't stand the idea of her going away, especially after I'd dreamt and planned every last detail. I was sure that everything would go smoothly. How could I be so wrong? Why did I lose control?

When I thought I was losing her for a second time, I tried, on impulse, to prevent it at any cost. I was willing to do anything. Curiously, I didn't feel any aggressiveness towards her; I didn't want to mistreat her or cause her any physical harm. The only thing that I can remember is that I desired her to death. She defended herself, but I didn't believe her heart was really in it, at least at the outset. Then, all of a sudden she became powerful and threw me to the floor with surprising strength.

It was then that I had my second unexpected reaction. I felt that there was nothing I could do. She really didn't want to do "it". She was rejecting me. And instead of feeling anger or disappointment, instead of opening the door to tell her to get the hell out of here, I felt an immense desolation, and deep exhaustion. As if I had been abandoned alone in the world. Could it have anything to do with the fact that her name is Elida? That is idiotic and makes no sense at all.

The truth of the matter is that I took off all my clothes; I lay down on the couch, and I stayed there with my eyes closed. I had no idea what was going to happen. I did see how she turned to stone when she saw me naked: a vulgar exhibitionist. I can't explain why I did it. Anyway, it worked. When she saw that I was weak and passive, she decided to stay. And she did more than stay; she caressed me with such a modest tenderness that I was moved. That must be what caused me to live the most intense, explosive pleasure I've experienced in years.

I should consider it a victory. Indeed, it was, if I analyze it as the result of a strategic maneuver. But that wasn't the case. I suspect the victory was hers.

## Chapter Thirteen

### *Kangaroo for Two*

He had just gotten home when the doorbell rang. He ran to the intercom with a hunch that it was her. He had not stopped thinking about her since the night before. He reacted to all the demands of daily life as if he were on automatic pilot so that he could completely enjoy his sweet and bitter obsession. In the intervals between his daydreams, he kept coming back to the same questions: When will I see her again? Will I look for her? The moment he heard the doorbell, he knew it was her; he was relieved and thankful that it was, like a convalescent who can see the final cure for his illness.

"Yes," he answered.

"It's me, Elida..."

"Come in," Andrés replied without letting her say anything else.

He had to admit that he was anxious and excited. The vision of her naked body, in his dreams, erupted in his brain like an intermittent flash. When he opened the door, the first thing he noticed was that she was wearing jeans. A bad sign—for sure—but she looked marvelous with her long legs and narrow waist. He stared at her in an obvious way so that she would notice his admiration.

"You look terrific in jeans!"

As he closed the door he had the opportunity to observe her from behind. She's incredible! He told himself with joy, and besides, she's come back on her own account. Now it's my turn to play hard to get. I have to go slow.

"Have a seat. Would you like something to drink?"

"No thanks, I just ate."

Andrés sat down a prudent distance from her.

"How are things? How's work?"

"Okay. I still haven't handed in my resignation, but one of these days I will."

"Tell me something, why do you want to quit? Aren't you happy there? Don't they pay you enough?"

"That's not the problem. It's infuriating. To think that an inefficient institution full of apathetic people can solve such a complex problem is crazy."

"Yes, of course, bureaucracy," Andrés added.

"Among other things."

And then a notable silence. Elida rolled and unrolled the strap of her purse. Andrés remembered her caresses. Oh how I desire to tell her about it! But she's the one who's come back. He would let her speak. Finally, after coughing twice, she continued:

"I've been thinking about what happened last night. I think we should put everything out on the table."

Andrés smiled to himself and remained silent.

"As I told you before, I'm going through a difficult time. I can't think straight; I have so many decisions to make and that scares me. Okay?"

Andrés remained attentive and silent. He would not go along with her. He felt he was in a strong position and was not going to give it up.

"I'm saying this so that you won't take my reaction last night seriously. I'm not interested in starting a relationship with anyone. I don't want to have anything to do with that for a long time."

Elida became quiet. Andrés looked at her, not believing a word she had said. She wouldn't have come here just to tell me that, although she's probably not aware of her feelings. Nonetheless, he decided that it was not the right moment for him to set her straight.

"Have you heard that phrase that the yogis chant?" Elida said, breaking her silence. "The carnal path leads to death. I'm disappointed with that kind of relationship. Sooner or later, you end up suffering. If you want to be friends, that's fine."

Andrés got comfortable in the armchair and lit a cigarette. It was a demand shared by many of the women that he had met. What they really wanted was to assure the permanence of the relationship without having to risk a thing; it was their way of beating around the bush so it would not look like a trap. Similar to what his mother had proposed to him on his twenty-third birthday, when he announced for the last time that he was going to live elsewhere. That's fine, but keep coming twice a week, come for lunch on Sundays, and besides, she didn't have to add, I need the money that you give me twice a month. He would take advantage of her offer, but he would not fall into her trap.

"As you wish," Andrés answered. "But anyway, I'd like to tell you that it was an unforgettable experience."

He noticed that she avoided his eyes. He wished that everything could be easier, that she could be different, even though her name was Elida. He would like to sit down close to her and embrace her without any explanations. That woman really turned him on. He expressed his feelings spontaneously:

"It's going to be difficult to forget about what happened. Indeed, I haven't stopped thinking about you since last night. I didn't think I was going to see you again."

"I just wanted to clarify our situation," Elida responded, sensing an accusatory tone in his voice.

"Well, I appreciate it. Now, if you'll excuse me, I'm expecting company," he said as he got up from the couch.

Elida stood up at once.

"Of course... Excuse me for barging in on you, but I didn't know how to get in touch with you."

"I understand, don't worry about it. If you want, I'll give you my telephone number in case you need anything," Andrés replied in the most neutral manner he could affect.

"That's okay, thanks."

As they were saying goodbye, Andrés surprised her with a tender, sweet kiss on her cheek. She noticed that he stayed at the doorway up to the last minute.

Elida went home mulling over the ball of contradictions that were bothering her. She had said and done exactly what she had planned. He had taken everything very well. He had said goodbye in a polite manner at the door. Why then, this uneasy feeling? Why the dark butterflies in her stomach? Why that foolish rage towards Andrés she tries but cannot hide?

When she enters her apartment, it seems so monstrously empty to her. I have to bring my plants from mother's house, she says to herself, hang some ferns, buy some posters, perhaps a batik sarong with many warm colors. She says this in order to convince herself that it is the solution: to act, to do things, and to interact with people.

She could have asked her mother or Federico how they manage to live alone. How does one do it, how does one do it, she repeats these words to fill her emptiness, how does one do it? She would like to write it down anywhere, on a billboard, on the door of a public bathroom or on her living-room wall, and why not? It could be interesting and useful to have a place to write these kinds of things, things we like and things we hate.

And Andrés, she wondered, how can he live alone?

Elida sat down. She had understood the origin of her malaise: her visit with Andrés. He was not alone because he was expecting company he would welcome the same way he had welcomed her, the same way he had welcomed so many other women, the indiscriminate parade of women in which each one occupied her place in line on a provisional basis only. And far from feeling envious, she felt sorry for those women and for herself.

And it suddenly occurred to her that men are never alone because their hearts are like reception rooms where new and old guests come and go.

This idea amused her and she laughed. Since she felt much better, she concluded that in order to live alone, she would have to learn to laugh alone. After laughing, as she tossed and turned in her bed trying to fall asleep, and later, in the early morning, after sleep had shown her all of desire's tricks, Elida remembered Andrés again. She pictured for herself the last vision of him that had remained engraved in her mind: Andrés, standing by his door, his left hand in his pants pocket, his right arm against the frame of the door, his body leaning slightly to one side.

She reviewed his oblique image against the light, which created a tenuous glow around his body. She took special joy in the look in his eyes. A look that seemed to project silk threads that wrapped around her. Elida repeated over and over again the kiss that disturbed her with unexpected and gratuitous warmth. And she gave in to the temptation of thinking that that look and that kiss belied the long line, the dates, the multiple, the provisional, in order to be part of the magic space of the unique and irreplaceable.

## Chapter Fourteen

### *Anteater*

Elida spent a long morning at work; she was both absent and distracted. She imparted, however, inexplicable glances of affection to the people around her.

The difficulty she had experienced over the past few months in meeting even the slightest demands of her job seemed to have evaporated. Life, having acquired a symbolic face, became beautiful and bearable.

She accepted the dubious friendliness of her fellow workers who had tried shamelessly to hit on her since they learned of her divorce.

Even the salacious glances of the boss of her department seemed less nauseating. She even allowed herself to smile at that man's insinuations; he embodied all the characteristics that Elida detested the most: he was clumsy, obese, and machista, the multiple prejudices that had been reinforced in Elida because she had run into all those characteristics together with great frequency.

She was looking through the file of ongoing cases with a complacent lethargy when her phone rang. It was her boss calling from the main office.

That enormous woman, with curly, slightly graying hair, welcomed her with a big smile. Elida smiled too, because it took no effort on her part, although she could not avoid the premonition that trouble was brewing.

"Elida, how are things? Please sit down," she said in the direct and unequivocal manner that characterized her. "You must be wondering why I called you. You seem to me a very competent, responsible, and loyal person. That's why I thought about making you a proposition that I'm sure you're going to like."

She pulled out a thick folder from her file cabinet and took some papers from it which she spread out on her desk. She leaned back in her chair and continued:

“For the past several months, I have been meeting and discussing some matters with Dr. Maroto, the Assistant Secretary of Health, Professor Vargas, the Director of the Children’s Institute, our nation’s first lady and her advisors in charge of the Program to Assist Abandoned, Abused, and Addicted (glue-sniffing) Children. I’ve also had discussions with Dr. Alba, of the Attorney General’s Office for Juvenile Matters, Professor Juan José Oconitrillo, from the National Youth Institute, Mr. Roger Vindas, the National Coordinator of Community Associations of the National Directorate for Rural Development, and with Eugenia Bunker, the Head of Cultural Promotion for the Ministry of Culture.

Elida found the long list of titles, names, and government departments somewhat bewildering; she didn’t know whether to memorize the information, as a kind of challenging game, or simply to listen.

“The idea is to create an inter-institutional program throughout the country to help prevent addiction to alcohol and other drugs among our youth.”

“But Isabel, isn’t that the job of...?”

“We should be responsible for that program,” her boss interrupted firmly. “It’s our department’s duty to bring together the dispersed efforts of all the organizations involved, to centralize the administration of resources, and to assure the continuation of the program. I’ve already discussed it with Dr. Rubén Maroto. We worked closely together in the last administration, and a bill, which is already being drafted, will be introduced in the National Assembly by one of our representatives. That law provides for the channeling of existing resources and the creation of new fiscal revenues to finance the program.”

Elida remained silent in the face of the movement of such imposing political machinery. At that moment, Elida remembered with surprise real parades from the stories of her childhood, parades, which were always presided over by pot-bellied tax collectors. Could it be a defense mechanism? She immediately put aside those foolish associations so she could continue listening to her boss.

“This is a very opportune moment for us,” she continued. The present government needs to address criticisms from the press and get ahead of possible initiatives from the opposition. We are in the pre-campaign period.”

"Yes, of course," Elida answered, thinking to herself: When aren't we?

"I need somebody who's loyal, to whom I can entrust a program with so much responsibility. And I thought of you."

Elida looked at her with surprise, not knowing what to say. She had the feeling that it was more of a trap than an opportunity for her to say yes or no. Far from feeling praised, the idea overwhelmed her.

"I wasn't expecting this," she finally answered. "As a matter of fact, Isabel, to be honest, I've been thinking about turning in my resignation."

"How could you even think such a thing, Elida? How long have you been in this department?

"Six years."

"Six years...! And you have been able to adapt to the new changes we have instituted since the change of government. You are efficient and you work well with your colleagues. The head of your department has only great things to say about you."

"Why didn't you offer the position to him?"

"Well, you know Mr. Ramírez is planning to retire soon. And besides, he's a difficult person to work with, he's not qualified for this assignment, and his ideas are outdated. Just between you and me, Elida, you know as well as I do that Mr. Ramírez has kept his position only because of connections he has with some members of the leadership of the political party in power."

"I'm grateful that you have considered me for the position, but I'll need to think about it. It'd be hard for me to make a decision right now," Elida replied.

"That's fine, think it over. But it's a great opportunity for you. You'd receive a considerable increase in salary, along with a stipend and travel allowance. Now that you live alone, you probably have more expenses."

"How do you know I live alone?" Elida said with increasing surprise.

"We know everything; we're like one big family here. I heard that you got a divorce, and that you don't get any alimony... Believe me, I'd love to help you. I've been there before."

Elida looked at her with skepticism. All too often, she had experienced the painful lack of solidarity among women. Her boss's attitude conflicted with the old pattern of distrust. And, since it is hard to break with old patterns, Elida tried to guess the hidden motives behind her offer: What's in it for her? Isabel interrupted her thoughts.

"It's almost twelve. How about lunch at the Chinese restaurant next door? That way we can talk a little more. I have to make a couple of phone calls, so we'll meet at the restaurant at a quarter after twelve."

"Okay, see you there."

Back in her office, Elida sat down and remained still for a long while. She thought long and hard about the offer she had just received. The names, titles, and words continued to resonate in her mind until they lost their meaning, like in a children's song. And she, like a translucent jellyfish, felt herself floating on the long row of desks and file cabinets. She saw her boss greeting her. And there, beside her, was Andrés's naked body on a deep green lawn, and a little farther away, was Federico, surrounded by a mountain of books.

The sound of the bell announcing lunchtime brought her back to reality. She picked up her purse and left the office. When she punched her time card, she wondered why it was so difficult for her to relate to things having to do with her own life. She sighed as she thought about the determination and energy of women like her boss.

At the Chinese restaurant, most of the tables were occupied. There was one available next to the door to the kitchen. Elida sat down to wait. She observed the people: several colleagues from work that greeted her at the door, the unmistakable young fellows in coat and tie from the Protestant seminary, a couple of mechanics from the garage on the corner. Everyone seemed to move and speak in surprising harmony: the same feeling one would get watching an anthill. When her boss arrived, Elida thought that she was the queen of the ants. When she sat down in front of her, the Chinese waitress immediately came with the menu.

"I'm going to try the chop suey; it's their specialty, and a tamarind juice."

"What are you having, Elida?"

Elida noticed a reassuring tone of familiarity in her boss's words.

"I'll have the same thing you're having; I love chop suey."

"Where are you living these days?"

"Near Sabanilla. I rented an apartment."

"That's a pretty area." She was silent for a moment and then asked: "How are you feeling?"

Elida did not know how to answer such an abrupt and open question.

"Well, I feel pretty good," Elida answered with a duplicitous smile.

"I know that it's not easy for a woman to get a divorce and to live by herself. Fortunately, you don't have any children."

Without wanting to, Elida was distracted for a moment by the memory of Federico's obstinate opposition whenever she would bring up the subject of having a baby. She voluntarily closed that door to the past and continued listening to her boss.

"...to place three sons on the right track. My two older ones are working now, and the youngest is at the university."

"You didn't remarry?"

"Oh, no. No way!" she answered with a big grin.

"Why not?"

"Men in this country still look at a wife as a good investment: they prepare their food, wash their clothes, wait on them, got to bed with them... everything, gratis. And on top of that, when they run into a young girl that revives their ego, they do everything they can to get rid of their wives without offering them any financial support."

Elida laughed heartily at such an unexpected explanation. In a certain way, she enjoyed that fresh appraisal, one free of prejudice and so distant from melodramatic ones.

All afternoon she thought more about the things her boss had said than about the job offer, as if acceptance of that new position required the adoption of a new style: a rational, dispassionate, intensively business-like approach.

# Chapter Fifteen

## *Impossible Syntheses*

Elida walked slowly on her way home. She used her parasol as a walking cane in order to maintain an elegant and harmonious gait as she negotiated the poorly maintained sidewalks that were cluttered with multicolored bags of garbage that had been discarded along the street.

The images of Andrés and her boss alternated with the movement of a capricious pendulum.

She had accepted an invitation from a small group of her coworkers who, after work, often went somewhere together for a beer. Among the male members of the group there were married, single, and divorced men as well as one widower. All the females were either single or divorced. It was the first time she had accepted their invitation because now she felt that she met the requirement and common denominator of the group: she was available.

When the stoplight turned green, she thought about the job offer again. It could be an opportunity to reorganize her life around a task and not around dreams as was her habit. She pictured herself in a spacious office, in front of a desk covered with papers and several telephones, her agenda full of appointments with important people, and, all of a sudden, the image of a man breaks into the center of the scene. Weakened by the apparition of that shadow, she thought that she was not cut out to be a bureaucrat or to fight for a position in the formal networks of power. What was she good for then? For sitting behind a small desk with just one telephone? For taking orders? Small-time bureaucracy? A small job that allowed her to survive between dreams without a guilty conscience. What good was it to dream if there was no love in her life? Why hadn't she been successful in love? Why did the memory of Andrés keep coming back with such persistence?

When she turned the street corner, the first thing she saw was Andrés's window with a light on. He was there, perhaps thinking about her.

She took her time, but she knew that when she got to the gate she would be unable to resist the temptation to ring his apartment.

"Vicky?" Andrés answered.

Elida remained still. She did not respond again when Andrés asked who was there. Trying to ignore the painful feeling of ridicule, she continued walking towards her apartment. At the exact moment she was going to go in, a black pearl-colored car, with license plates that read MINE, stopped a few yards ahead of her. A woman got out of the car. When she saw her enter Andrés's building, she was absolutely certain that she was Vicky, the company that Andrés was expecting.

Back in her apartment, Elida was sorry she had not stayed longer at the bar with the group from her office. What was there to do in that empty apartment? SOLITUDE, spelled in capital letters, feeling oneself alone, unique and unable to communicate with the world, was more bearable than her small domestic solitude, the impossibility of sharing her day to day existence with someone else. Maybe if she were completely exhausted from work, satisfied with her daily labor, she would not feel that emptiness. Maybe she ought to accept that position, even knowing that it would be painful to live in a world of official appearances. Or perhaps, with time, she would come to firmly believe in the pompous phrases that appeared in the mission statements of all governmental organizations. The magic meaning of slogans seemed to be contagious in the highest spheres of bureaucracy.

Would it be better to resign and do something else as she had been planning to do over the past few weeks? And what else could she do if all her work experience, and her life experience, had transpired under the shadow of protective institutions? She did not like domestication, but she wasn't sure about the alternative. Most of the time Elida knew precisely what she did not want. It was only confusing to her when it came to deciding what she really wanted. Since this second alternative was not clear, she learned to base her decisions on the first criterion, that is, by saying no to those things she did not want. "I don't want to live with Federico anymore," so they got a divorce without Elida having given any thought as to what she would do in the future. Her supreme power consisted, sometimes, in just saying no.

From the corner where she had curled up, Elida saw the disorganized books on the shelves. She felt like rereading a text that she remembered at that moment. She searched among the volumes for Hawthorne's little red book. She returned to the corner and began to leaf through its pages until she found the passage she was looking for in the prologue. It was about the government worker who had lost his job:

> *Conscious of his own infirmity—that his tempered steel and elasticity are lost—he looks wistfully about him forever afterwards in quest of support external to himself. His pervading and continual hope—a hallucination, which, in the face of all discouragement, and making light of impossibilities, haunts him while he lives, and, I fancy, like the convulsive throes of the cholera, torments him for a brief space after death—is, that finally, and in a short time, by some happy coincidence of circumstances, he shall be restored to office. This faith, more than anything else, steals the pith and availability out of whatever enterprise he may dream of undertaking. Why should he toil and moil, and be at so much trouble to pick himself up out of the mud, when, in a little while hence, the strong arm of his Uncle will raise and support him? Why should he work for his living here, or go to dig gold in California, when he is so soon to be made happy, at monthly intervals, with a little pile of glittering coins from his Uncle's pocket?*
>
> *It is sadly curious to observe how slight a taste of office suffices to infect a poor fellow with this singular disease. Uncle Sam's gold—meaning no disrespect to the worthy old gentleman—has, in this respect, a quality of enchantment like that of the devil's wages. Whoever touches it should look well to himself, or he may find the bargain to go hard against him, involving, if not his soul, yet many of its better attributes; its sturdy force, its courage and constancy, its truth, its self-reliance, and all that gives the emphasis to manly character.*

Elida smiled when she finished reading the text. There appeared to be no difference between the bureaucrats of the nineteenth century and those of her own twentieth century.

If she left her comfortable niche as a public employee, what could she do? She imagined herself floundering in nostalgia for the past just like the Jews in the desert who longed for the onions of Egypt after they had gained their freedom.

Had she not felt nostalgia for Federico at some point, a longing for the boundaries of a life and a house "in order"? Were not loneliness and helplessness odious?

## Chapter Sixteen

### *The Power of Desire*

Andrés had enough time to see the whole thing from his window. And he was delighted. Deep inside he did not consider this coincidence to be quirk of fate but rather the consequence of the force of his allure. A manifestation of his hidden power over women that filled him with satisfaction.

After he talked with Elida, he could not wait until Monday to get together with Vicky. He could see in Elida's eyes, when he last saw her from the landing on the staircase, that she would return. But he did not want to wait. That is why he looked for another woman. It was a great remedy to help alleviate tension and to eliminate the feeling of boredom. He made a date with Vicky for that very night, and now he would enjoy their encounter twice as much because Elida knew about it.

For that reason, when he embraced Vicky with excessive desire, when he rocked her surrender with waves of learned tenderness, when they ran naked throughout the house like crazy people and laughed without stopping like children, when Vicky wrapped herself around him with arms and legs like those of a sweet carnivorous plant, when they made love until they could no longer do so, Andrés could not—nor did he want to—stop feeling Elida's eyes watching them from a dark corner of her abandonment.

Andrés rested his head on Vicky's lap. He enjoyed the fatigue after an extenuating evening. When she was not looking, he checked the alarm clock on the night stand and saw that it was almost two o'clock in the morning. He sat up and yawned in an exaggerated fashion.

"Sweetheart," he said to Vicky, "a coworker from the lab is coming here very early tomorrow. We have to finish writing an urgent report for our boss. We had planned to work on it tonight, but I couldn't resist the temptation of being with you."

Vicky sat up and looked at his shifty eyes. It did not surprise her. She had known Andrés for a long time and she knew that he always worked it out so that no woman spent the night at his place or attempted, the following morning, to prepare his breakfast as if they were married. At one time she tried to do that. Now she smiled because she was no longer interested and Andrés's fear seemed a little ridiculous to her.

"If you want, I'll go with you so you won't be alone," he added in a solicitous tone that rang hollow.

"Don't bother, honey. Grace's house it just ten minutes from here. Nothing will happen to me."

He watched her go into the bathroom and then he heard the sound of the shower. It's always an advantage when they've got a car, Andrés thought.

When Vicky kissed him goodbye, Andrés curled up in his blanket feeling everything was perfect. Vicky was a fabulous woman. Tomorrow he would open the second file in his dossier.

He heard the sound of her car driving away until it disappeared. Now he could sleep to his heart's content, satisfied, at peace, knowing that, when he woke up the following morning, he would find no one in his exclusive bachelor's bed.

Nonetheless, Elida's image surprised him in the instant before he fell asleep. I wonder what she's doing. He imagined her alone in her bed, awake, thinking about him, longing for him, and he could not avoid feeling that it was a waste. For a moment, he wanted to hold her in his arms and kiss her in his dreams, softened by that inclination he had fought against so hard, not to feel tenderness towards the women who longed for him.

## Chapter Seventeen

*File #2*

Andrés was content. The joy of a spectacular night followed him around like a benevolent shadow. Certain images exploded in his memory with an unexpected intensity. They intruded with such a sudden force that Andrés felt himself being transported to another dimension. Then a vague arousal ran throughout his whole body.

Apart from those moments of escape, Andrés maintained a friendly relationship with reality. Love making increased Andrés's vitality, gave him a zest for living that made his work more pleasant and conversations with his friends more enjoyable, and made him thankful for his lot in life.

Even his tolerance came out unscathed when, upon arriving at the office, his coworkers gave him the latest news: on the recommendation of the Great Dane, smoking in the building had been prohibited, except in a small room next to the cafeteria. Morning found all the walls of the building covered with grim signs that promised death to anyone who smoked.

The non-smokers strolled through the halls and offices with a triumphant smile on their faces.

"Not even in the cafeteria, man that's crazy!" one of Andrés's coworkers protested.

"Well, anyway, tobacco causes impotence," Andrés answered, willing to see the positive side of everything that day.

"You have sex on your brain!" his coworker responded with a swift obscene gesture.

"And how many times can we go to the smoking area?" Andrés asked.

"During the coffee break, at lunch, and when you have to take a leak, what assholes!"

Since it was the first day of prohibition, the smoking lounge was filled with vengeful smokers who were lighting up one cigarette after another, polluting the air to the point where it was impossible to breath. And since the restrooms were at the rear of the smoking lounge, the smokers had the opportunity to make fun of all the people that had to cut through that tide of smoke in order to get to them.

"What is this shit!" the head of accounting protested as she waved her hands like fans in the air.

"They should give you a gasmask with every roll of toilet paper!" a smoker shouted with derision.

It was an entertaining day and Andrés wanted to end it at the corner bar before going home. While he was chatting with a couple of acquaintances, to inspect the terrain he cast several glances at the few women who were there at that time. Andrés had no intention of taking a woman home with him that night. It was just his habit of always remaining alert in case something extraordinary were to pop up.

That was not the case, however, so he finished his drink and leisurely walked home, jumping over the puddles of water from the afternoon rain, enjoying the orange sunset of the rainy season. He could not wait to get home to start his second file. It was like a delightful ghost: a double of Vicky.

Before he entered his apartment, he looked at Elida's building, at her apartment window. There was a slight anxiety in his stomach, as he told himself, "I hope she thought about me all last night, I hope she was jealous," making him realize that his date with Vicky had not expelled Elida from the obsessive corner of his heart where she appeared to have taken up permanent residence.

While he was changing his wet shoes, he made an effort to think about Vicky, her soft body writhing between his legs, her large, rounded hips. He wanted to relive the excitement of that moment so he could impart that tone in his writing of her file. He had already accomplished this before he sat down to work. Fantasy was often his main sexual organ. He took the folder and wrote Victoria Ballesteros Luna in his secret code of letters and numbers:

/ B3 / L9 / V5 /

Vicky was perfect for the dossier, Andrés thought. He knew everything there was to know about her. He had tasted, measured, and enjoyed just about every inch of her. He could fill in all her information, answer any question about her. There was no mystery here.

As a general rule, for Andrés, that spelled the end of his amorous relationships. Sooner or later, his interest in a woman inevitably declined once they got to know each other well. Once his ardent anxiety—to experience, to know in the Biblical sense, to master the mystery—was satisfied, his desire turned into disgust. That is why it was necessary for him to continue his search for new oases. No orgy, no erotic or sentimental disappointment, could eliminate that impulse in him.

But Vicky's case was different. He had the incomparable advantage of distance. She had remained an "open file" for more than eight years. During that time, they had seen each other about ten times. Enough time passed between their "dates" to keep the excitement of something new and the frenzy of their previous encounter alive.

It was like that right from the beginning. As he remembered that day, Andrés smiled. With the composure of a collector who knows he has discovered a great find, he started to write. He took a long time delighting in the minutest details: birthmarks and moles, her measurements, her passion for Latin American music, the Tarot and astrological cards, her demagogic heart of a Leo, her salary in dollars, and her passion for marihuana, whisky, and men.

When he got to the second section, Andrés hesitated briefly, without knowing where to begin. It was like trying to choose just one spot in a whirlwind of vitality.

He closed his eyes and tried to picture Vicky in his mind. What was the first thing he saw?

| 2. PERSONAL INFORMATION: |
|---|
| She's energetic, unsettled, uncontrollable, talkative, and enthusiastic. A whirlwind of fragrances and colors. Her hair is wild—as if it were charged with electricity on the tips. She wears several necklaces at the same time, tons of bracelets, long earrings that swing by her neck—silver rings that flash in the air. She likes to wear loose clothing: baggy skirts and blouses. She loves sandals, shawls, scarves, and ponchos. On special occasions, she dresses in Indian silk. But the curious thing about the way she dresses is not the kind of clothing she wears, the fascinating thing is that no matter what she wears, she always has that sloppy look, a kind of wild abandon, as if she never ironed her clothes, brushed her hair or used makeup. The Brigitte Bardot look.<br><br>There are no barriers with Vicky, at least that's what I think. She looks like she just got out of bed or is ready to go there in a heartbeat. That, along with her fabulous hips, her incredible cleavage, her nightclub laugh, give her a provocative air of immediate availability and make her irresistible even though she's not pretty. She is an erotic torrent that sweeps away, that entraps, as she did to me that morning when she came to spread suntan lotion on me. |

When he had finished writing this section, Andrés slowly reread the text. There were two peculiar things about Vicky that had always intrigued him: her age and her lack of beauty. It was not like Andrés was a fanatic about beauty. He liked beautiful women, of course, but he did not lose any sleep over them. Curiously, he almost enjoyed desiring them more than possessing them. When he was young, there was a time when he would not miss any opportunity to be seen in public with a spectacular woman. It did not matter whether it was because of their physical appearance, attire, or nationality, the women who accompanied him had to create a sensation. That is the way he established his reputation.

Andrés had heard that women are attracted to men who are loved by beautiful women. The important thing about them was not having a relationship with them but being seen with them. He never took them very seriously. It was his conviction that beauty requires an excessive quota of force and effort for protection, and he was not interested in that kind of servitude. His reputation as a Don Juan lady-killer grew when it became public knowledge that he had rejected the advances of a beautiful woman who was crazy about him.

Generally, he also avoided ugly and insignificant women. Not only for the damage they could inflict upon his reputation, but also because he perceived in them a greater propensity for possessiveness and jealousy, an unhealthy adoration for the man who paid any attention to them.

All in all, it was hard for Andrés to turn his nose up at a woman. His expert erotic eye allowed him to discover in almost all of them that particular detail that released his desire. In Vicky's case, Andrés captured from the first moment her vital strength, her initiative, her love for life and pleasure, and her intense sexuality.

Another curious detail was her age. Vicky was four years older than him and right now was forty-four. In his youth, Andrés had also sought out older women. At seventeen he had girlfriend who was twice his age. One day he took her home to present her to his father. It was like saying to him: look at her, take a good look at her, and you thought I was a dolt, but I too can have a real woman. The old man threw them out of the house, but Andrés left feeling satisfied, like a person who finally closes the door to a cesspit.

Over time, Andrés got over that fetish, and the day came when he had no specific preference when it came to age. He remained in a comfortable zone of equilibrium. He neither pursued young girls, as Chaplin did, nor did he seek out women in their forties, like Burt Reynolds or George Hamilton.

From experience, he was able to deduce that the ideal age for a woman was between twenty-five and thirty-five: the high tide of feminine libido. He remembered Elida with uneasiness. But he never let any form of age prejudice keep him from enjoying both ends of the spectrum on occasion. And he smiled, remembering the sweet innocence of Cristina when she was sixteen.

When he met Vicky, he was thirty-two and she thirty-six. But that afternoon, in that small bathroom, Andrés felt that Vicky was ageless. She was, simply, a magnificent woman.

He picked up his pen and continued writing:

A. ENCOUNTER:

I really hadn't paid attention to her. At that time, things were going well for me with Grace. We were spending a weekend in Tamarindo; Arturo and his friend Melba, Grace, the owner of the house, and myself. Vicky was friends with Grace, and since Vicky and her daughter were on vacation, she had invited them to the beach.

That's how I met her. I noticed her southern South American accent, her incessant blabbering. Of course I noticed her soft voluptuous body in that bathing suit, but I didn't really—really—check her out until she offered to rub suntan lotion on me.

The way she was looking at me left no room for doubt. Grace's presence—she was just a few yards away from us—made it even more exciting.

I don't know what kind of pressure or heat she had in her fingers, but her mere contact turned me on to such a degree that I had to conceal my lack of control by wrapping a towel around my waist.

She realized what had happened and started to laugh and make jokes. I don't like women who tell obscene jokes; I feel that they are invading my territory. But she did it in such a natural and humorous way, that she came off like a mischievous little girl.

I felt the heat of her eyes staring at me all afternoon. She took advantage of any and every opportunity to rub her body against mine, especially with her fabulous butt, her "tush" as Arturo would say.

Lying on the sand, I remember imagining how delightful it would be to sink between her thighs that were like living cushions.

I started to plan a way to be alone with her without Grace finding out.

But with Vicky, there's no need to think or to plan anything. She is the queen of improvisation both in and out of bed, any place or position is doable.

That same afternoon we did it in the bathroom as her little girl insistently pounded on the door. In the evening, we did it in Grace's jeep. Over the rest of the weekend, we didn't do it twice in the same place. The titillating excitement of having to hide, to run, and to keep an eye out was always present. It didn't take us more than five minutes. The expression "ladies come first" definitely applied to our situation. I had never felt so reconciled with my premature ejaculations as I did during those three days of madness.

I responded well to her voracity, as she let me know with great enthusiasm; however, my endurance has its limit. The one that lost out was Grace, who concluded at that time that I no longer loved her.

On Monday, Vicky returned to Uruguay, and I felt that I had held a shooting star in my hands.

B. AFFAIR:

Just like a shooting star, she passed through my life.

That kind of experience often leaves me dazed for a few days. It happened to me with Elida, even though it was only a brief encounter. But with Vicky, there was nothing, besides a general sense of satisfaction, that's for sure.

When I think about that encounter, it was if I had visited a bordello.

Sometimes I think it's true that feelings and sexual pleasure never come in the same package.

Every time I'm with Vicky it's like the fourth of July.

As long as it lasts, it's ecstasy. Then there's nothing. And I believe that that feeling—that there's nothing left—is what makes every rendezvous as passionate as the first time.

Vicky comes and goes. Without commitments or demands. We exploit and plunder one another by mutual consent. We absorb each other; we pervert each other without any trace of regret. Later, there is saturation, a happy, satisfied ending requiring no epilog.

We've probably been together some ten times during the past eight years or so; I'm not sure about the exact dates. It's too bad, because it would be interesting to recap all the distinct moments we spent together, where and what time of the year, the unpredictable and crazy ideas Vicky came up with.

I don't have a single souvenir from Vicky in my briefcase. There were no letters or phone calls between encounters. Nothing that smacked of permanence or continuity.

She is the perfect long-distance lover. With her it's like winning the sexual lottery every so often.

What an incredible woman that Vicky is! Although she is more woman than any woman I've ever known, she is the least feminine in her style. I've always had that same feeling about the few nymphomaniacs that I've known. The only difference is that Vicky enjoys herself to death; she doesn't put on an act. Her scandalous screaming comes from genuine pleasure.

Speaking of her screaming, on more than one occasion I've had to put my hand over her mouth, whenever the place she has hastily chosen was nothing short of highly inappropriate. A good example: in a movie theater, sitting on my lap during the matinee.

It's too bad that I didn't write down all our madcap adventures! It would make a great novel.

## Chapter Eighteen

### *Sentimental Rebirth at Forty*

Before going to work, Andrés opened his file cabinet and contemplated his files. Two in one week. It wasn't anything to shout about, but it wasn't bad either. He closed the drawer and left.

When he was about three hundred feet from the bus stop, he thought he saw Elida taking a taxi. The traffic light was red and the taxi stopped. He took off running as fast as he could. Why? How absurd! he said to himself, but he kept running nonetheless. He managed to see the gleam in her hair and the smooth line of her cheek before the taxi took off down the avenue.

He stood still, panting, until he lost sight of the taxi. He felt he had played the leading part in a scene from Doctor Zhivago: she was leaving and he could not do a thing about it.

He got in line in a sour mood. That woman and he could inspire a love story for a movie. And he remained like that all day long, as if he had been touched by a fairy.

During the coffee break, Andrés did not leave the laboratory.

"Hey dude, aren't you coming? You must be up to something..."

Sitting at a counter full of labeled bottles, he thought about his dossier. He remembered the scores he had assigned in his files. He gave a 10 to his encounter with Elida. A 7 or an 8 to Vicky. Why were Vicky's scores so low if he had such a wild time with her?

It seemed like an interesting idea to try to analyze those aspects of his relationship with Vicky that led him to give her such low scores. He picked up a piece of paper and wrote: Negative aspects of my relationship with Vicky. First of all, she was the one who came after me, and I prefer to choose the woman I want.

Is that possible? Even though he did not have files to verify his hypothesis, he could go so far as to declare that he had the best time with the women he had chosen, worked hard to get, and seduced on his own initiative.

What a shame he had not started his dossier right at the beginning. If he had, he would be able to confirm whether or not the scores he had given for "Encounter" were higher when he had taken the initiative. He could also correlate the relationship between the scores for "Encounter" and "Affair." Despite so many lost memories, Andrés was sure that there was a positive connection between them. The most satisfying affairs, without a doubt, would be the ones he had initiated.

He lamented the shortsightedness—the exclusive interest in the present—of his youth, which had limited his possibilities in the field of love. He never imagined that a diary or a dossier could be an erotic investment for old age. Did not the black briefcase offer him solace in his moments of loneliness and low self-esteem?

He reread the first point, and after thinking about it for a while, he continued writing. Secondly, she talks too much in bed, she says too much and I find that distracting.

To enjoy a woman completely, Andrés needed to concentrate on his physical sensations, the images, he needed to contemplate her and himself. That was why he never liked to drink or take drugs of any kind when he took someone to bed. This practice had given him unique opportunities with the female companions of his friends and acquaintances who ended up drunk at parties. Women always prefer to make love with sober men, and fortunately Andrés also preferred to remain sober. He needed to maintain all his faculties. And Vicky's non-stop chatting forced him to pay attention to what she was saying, diminishing his capacity to feel.

He lit a cigarette, having forgotten the Nordic prohibition against smoking. He was thinking about Elida, about the intensity of her silent gaze. She had not said a word when he undressed himself and lay down on his couch. Nor had she uttered a sound when she was caressing him. There was only that intense fiery look in her eyes that now made him close his eyes so that he could remember hers better.

He returned to reality and continued writing.

Third: A kind of emptiness, a nostalgia for the feeling of being in love.

He had never experienced the absence of love like he had on his last date with Vicky. It was so wonderful to be in love! He missed the magic, the element of mystery, of being moved. Even his soul trembled. He remembered that after they were done he deeply desired for her to leave.

Andrés thought, for the second time in a few days that, without a doubt, being in his forties had really taken a toll on him. He remembered the indirect attack Vicky had made on him in a humorous way: "Darling, you're falling behind. I'm going to have to trade you in for two twenty-year olds."

There was no love, Vicky was just using him. It was not the first time he had thought about it, but it was the first time that it made him sad. He saw himself diminished, weakened, less successful and less well-off financially, and less educated than her.

Could it be that Vicky's bizarre theory was right? The ideal couple for a woman is when she is in her forties and her young man in his twenties; and for a man, when he is in his fifties and the young woman is fifteen.

Andrés was lost in thought for a moment trying to imagine how many couples in the world with those specifications would be possible and how long would they last. Then he thought about young girls, a very young one, how long has it been since I've had one, he thought.

As a general rule, young girls did not appeal to him. He did not particularly care for playing the deer hunter or the high-school teacher who tries to impress his young pupil with any old worn-out trick. He was not cut out to be a Pygmalion. He preferred women with strong personalities, independent women, women who had initiative and money.

But he had to admit that recently he was especially moved by the sight of a young thing in short shorts, riding her bicycle down the street. It made him feel like running right after her, following her and catching up with her.

Did his need for passion and tenderness have anything to do with being in his forties? What did the obsessive memory of Elida have to do with all this?

Andrés compared the feelings he had felt when he was with Elida with the ones he had with Vicky. On some level that he could not identify, the difference was enormous. That magnetic tension that came over him when he was near Elida, that painful and sharp desire to possess her and to be possessed by her, could it be because he had yet to possess her?

## Chapter Nineteen

### *The Magic Law*

The law of simultaneity, which appears to manipulate the strings of fate, precipitated events in such a way that when Elida was going to the pharmacy at 7:20 in the evening to buy some Betadine for a burn on her hand that occurred when she was preparing her dinner, Andrés was saying goodbye to a well-dressed man in front of his apartment building. The man was smiling as he handed Andrés some keys and then left in a car with a woman—at least someone with a large head of flashy, red hair—who had been waiting for him.

There they ran into each other. Elida told him about her burn and Andrés offered her some silver sulfadiazine, an excellent product that they used in his laboratory for burns.

Elida accepted his offer because its logic justified it without forcing her to recognize that she had other motives.

Back in the apartment, a tremendous mess was waiting for them. Elida saw immediately that the bed was undone and there were wet towels on the floor. She remembered the couple in the car and the keys that that man had handed to Andrés.

"It appears that your friends are a little messy."

Andrés did not say a thing. With an angry gesture, he picked up the bedspread and the towels and put them in a plastic bag that he left in the bathroom. Then he took a sheet from the closet and spread it over the bed. As he was opening the door to a small patio, she heard him murmur: "That's the last time I'm letting that asshole use my apartment." Then he went back to Elida.

"Please forgive this chaos, here's the ointment."

He opened a black jar and he rubbed some cool, oily cream on her burn that soothed the pain. Elida was aware of every spot of her skin that Andrés touched. But the memory of his "guest" from last night and of the "couple" that had just departed left her divided as if a thin sheet of steel had split her in two.

"Would you care for a soft drink," Andrés kindly offered.

She accepted the soda and they both sat down on the same couch where they had been together the first time.

As she always did when something was bothering her, Elida addressed the topic:

"It looks to me like you run a dating service here."

"What makes you say that?"

"You let that couple use your apartment, didn't you?

"Well, yes, he's a good friend of mine," he answered, obviously uncomfortable with the direction their conversation had taken.

"And it wasn't the first time, from what I heard you say."

Andrés had not maintained the composure to lie, and, all of a sudden, he felt that there was no reason to do so. After all, was not he the master of his house and destiny?

"No, it wasn't the first time."

"And single women come to see you too."

He perceived a slight frown on Elida's lips. Then he understood that Elida was referring to Vicky. She was hurt. It was time to treat her with tenderness. He looked at her downcast head, the shadow of her eyelashes, her hands together on her lap, and he had the impulse to hug her. Instead he placed his hand on her shoulder.

"In the last few days, I've been interested in just one woman," he whispered to her.

Elida stood up. Standing in front of him, she started to speak as if she had opened an ancient gate inside her.

"I can't understand that indiscriminate search for sex. I can't understand it and it offends me that men have to have sexual relations with women as if they were objects, pieces of meat with no identity. It'd be like having sex with a goat or a chicken. It's obscene and repugnant."

"You're exaggerating, Elida," Andrés replied without taking her very seriously. There may be men like that. And it may be true that all men have acted that way at some point in their life. But that's not where I'm at. A woman interests me as a woman. That's the way it is; I like women very much. In fact, I could say I love them. I like to get to know them, find out what they're like and what they like. I need for them to enjoy themselves with me as much as I do with them. I'm not interested in raping anyone, even though what happened the other night—which was something out of character for me—might have you thinking the opposite. Each woman has something unique. They are all part of that essence of WOMANHOOD that attracts me like a magnet."

"But you like diversity, a collection. Not one of them is an individual person to you, but only a piece of that enormous sex object that you have in your head."

"At least I'm more realistic," Andrés responded in a defensive tone. I have an ideal woman in my head and I don't bug anyone with it, whereas you women pretend that every man you meet will be your ideal man, your perfect prince forever."

Elida stared at him with surprise. Then she said forcefully,

"That's right. It's only worth it to live and to make love with a man that incarnates that ideal. A man that we can admire, love, desire, and pamper..."

"That's impossible," Andrés interrupted her, "and unfair."

Elida noticed a slight tone of fatigue in his voice. Moved by a mixture of affection and curiosity, she put herself in his place for a second. Is it too much to ask of them? Could he be as weak as I am?"

They were silent for a few moments. Each one lost in thought, trying to put it all together, assimilating new information and unknown feelings, and remembering old loves.

They looked into one another's eyes. Each one penetrated the other to communicate without words that their disagreement had brought them closer together.

First, Andrés moved closer to her. He had picked up on a subtle difference in Elida's eyes that now revealed interest and expectation. He responded instinctively to that tacit command, to that fleeting second of magical understanding.

He slowly took her by her shoulders and pulled her towards himself.

They embraced in silence. He felt Elida's abandoned, soft body. He kissed her neck with tenderness. He saw her close her eyes, and watched how she let her head fall back, with her lips slightly parted. He heard her breathing and sighed softly. That marvelous transformation filled him with joy. Finally, that woman was his.

He picked her up in his arms and carried her to the bedroom. He put her down on the bed and, in between kisses and caresses, undressed her. Andrés decided that if she did not bring up the issue of whether or not to use a condom, he would not say a thing.

He remembered himself trying to imagine her body, which he now found to be even more beautiful and warmer than he had dreamt. And her fragrance of a timid kitten.

Elida did not move, her eyes were closed, and she shuddered with each new kiss, with each new caress.

She had always made love in silence and with her eyes closed. For her, it was an interior act, a relationship without intermediaries, with the most loved ghosts; her small steel core dilating without limit until it exploded with joy.

Her man was an invisible partner in that dark and silent world, an excuse to enter an indescribable delirium, one that is exclusively personal. A strong distrust kept her from sharing her feelings with a man. It had always been like that, and she never thought it could be any other way.

Until that day.

Andrés's voice brought down the hermetic walls of her passion. A magic voice, a plea and a command at the same time: "Look at me."

Elida responded to the spell and opened her eyes. When she saw him, she felt that it was the first time in her life that she was making love, the same dizziness, fear, shame, and under the same spell.

An acute awareness that they were two.

## Chapter Twenty

### *Sex Roles*

The following afternoon they saw each other again in Andrés's apartment. The conversation, coffee, and their beating-around-the-bush lead them back to the exchange of the previous night about themselves and pleasure. The haste of their desire left everything thrown about the living room, clothes everywhere. They made love leisurely and with tenderness, pausing at every peak to prolong the enjoyment of getting to know each other. Andrés's unquenchable desire fascinated her. And he was enthralled by Elida's capacity for pleasure: the sighs of a young girl hidden in her chest. A glance, any slight touch, an unexpected word, reignited the fire that was consuming them.

At the end of the night, they embraced one another in silence for a long time. The amorous struggle had left them more than exhausted, startled, and stunned. Elida kept embracing him firmly. How can I end this? What can I say?

Andrés was kissing her neck and repeating "Elida" softly. Then he slowly unglued himself from her body and Elida opened her arms and eyes as she felt that part of her skin was leaving with him. She saw him kneeling at the end of the bed. Spellbound, she observed his haughty and distant body as if under a spell; his flat shoulders were like an Egyptian sculpture. He had the demeanor of the inhabitants of the fortress, but his eyes sparkled with the brilliant complicity of a shared adventure.

Elida was disturbed by that brilliance, by that face that summed up in each of its traits the faces of all men: the strength and beauty of that body was the brilliant image, forever longed for, of MAN.

She closed her eyes the way she would facing an intense flash; the way they surrender to the excessive tenderness of a caress. She sighed deeply and her body seemed to expand without limit in the warm, humid air of the bedroom.

"Five!" Andrés whispered in her ear.

"Five?"

"That makes five deep sighs in the last ten minutes."

"Oh!"

They laughed at their misunderstanding; they embraced and tickled one another and ended up looking into each other's eyes, having surrendered to the tireless magnet that attracted their eyes.

"You make me sigh this way."

Andrés smiled with satisfaction and Elida congratulated herself for that smile. She confirmed that when she shared the language of seduction, she also shared power in the game of love.

She caressed his dark hair and rested her hand on the lovely curve of his neck. Andrés rubbed Elida's hand with a slight movement of his chin.

"You're like a spoiled cat," she told him with feeling.

He just purred when he felt her caresses again. And as she caressed him she thought he was the sweetest and most disconcerting man she had ever known. She felt that, in such a short period of time with him, she had learned more about herself than during the long years of deep introspection.

Over and over again she remembered with delight the firm, dark lines of his body entwined, blended together with hers, each one was the frame of reference and pleasure for the other. Then she closed her eyes and, as if she were playing a game with herself, assumed with satisfaction for the first time in her life her sexual role as a woman.

Andrés remained staring at her for a long time. He enjoyed the satisfied expression on her face.

"What's your Zodiac sign?" Andrés asked her with curiosity.

"Cancer, and yours?"

"Libra. We're both ruled by Venus."

"That's the only planet that revolves the other way around, did you know that?"

"I'm not surprised to hear that."

They laughed and Elida kissed him on his chest before getting up.

Andrés watched her as she walked naked towards the bathroom, and, performing a little pirouette as he got out of bed, he went to prepare coffee in the kitchen. While the water was being heated, Andrés slowly approached the bathroom door. Driven by a childish desire to spy, he slowly turned the doorknob. When he opened the door, he found her sitting on the toilet. Her body gave off a fragrance of bitter almonds. He apologized and closed the door. Walking slowly towards the kitchen, he said to himself:

"How can I like that woman so much!" He was so impressed by the way he felt, it was like discovering the ocean after a turn in the road.

That was what Andrés wrote in her file, once Elida had left. That he had never ever felt like he did with her, the unity of his whole being that was usually spread out among several relationships. Tenderness, passion, affection, friendship, and limitless desire.

That was what he had suspected the night he met her, when the harmonious fire in their eyes exploded. It wasn't just about pleasure; it was the unending desire to be with Elida, to kiss her, to look into her eyes as he caressed her. To feel that her desire remained even after the pleasure was gone, a desire of desire, infinite. To sink into Elida was like penetrating the soft flesh of a ripe peach. It was so pleasant to him that he yearned to remain there, still, inside her, to stay there forever. To die there.

## Chapter Twenty-One

### *Existential Imagination*

Elida was walking in a hurry. She had a lunch date with Andrés and she was late. The taxi had taken almost fifty minutes to cross the city from west to east. During the trip, she was lost in her thoughts and paid no attention to the taxi driver who cursed because Central Avenue had been closed to create a pedestrian shopping area, because the surrounding streets were under repair, because of the traffic jams, and because of the maddening, capricious games of the transit police.

The conversation with her boss about her divorce had left a bad taste in her mouth. She had felt as if another person were speaking for her. She had mixed feelings about saying anything bad about Federico. She remembered the peaceful feeling of security that she had experienced at his side. But also the loneliness of the wall that came between them when he lost himself in his books. A feeling that she needed air when she was locked up in the house with him.

"Let's go, Federico, let's go the movies or the theater. Can we go out to eat today? You can't spend every day stuck in your library, you have to go out and do something different."

Every day he became more entrenched in his cavern of misanthropy. Elida perceived in Federico's lifeless eyes an undercurrent of indifference, like the backwash on a beach after the tide has gone out. There remained only a coldness, which would only come to life with that well-known drive, as he silently laid the groundwork for a subsequent encounter in bed. Only then did his hands become tender, with a false tenderness, a bridge, a pretext, for a purely sexual encounter.

Elida longed for that other tenderness, when it had taken center stage in her fantasies about a lonely old man. She wanted it to be like it was in the beginning: to be in his arms, to sit on his lap, the cuddling, and the passion.

But that came to an end quickly. To maintain that relationship, they would have needed to have had a clear predisposition for incest. Elida had remembered the Sunday afternoons when Federico listened endlessly to Handel, the perfect music, he said, a state of harmony that God enjoyed before creating the universe. And she read without longing for anything. A kind of limbo.

"And now, hell?" Elida asked her boss. "Does this make any more sense?"

"Look, Elida, when one fails in life, he or she must kneel down in the gutter so that other more-foolhardy ones may pass. But we cannot let this make us feel that life is meaningless. It's a paranoiac temptation. We must realize that we're not imaginative enough."

It seemed strange for Elida to hear a bureaucrat talking about imagination, but she had to accept that she was right.

She had to go out, to have friends, to enjoy the company of men without expecting too much from them, her boss had told her. When we are young, we have the naïve hope of finding a man who will give us everything life has denied us or what we have been unable to obtain for ourselves, or what we have not dared to conquer for ourselves. "And that, Elida," she had told her, "is too much for any woman to withstand. We usually find that out much too late in life, when the struggle between our ghosts and reality has left us worn out. We waste so much energy! Men know how to play the game better because they don't dream as much as we do and they enjoy reality more."

Elida remembered the conversation she had had with Andrés about the same topic. In a certain way, he said the same things her boss was saying. She mentioned this to her, and they ended up talking for a long while about Andrés.

"How old is he?" her boss asked with interest, once Elida had finished sharing her most urgent personal secrets with her.

"He just turned forty."

"You're making the same mistake. You need to look for a man your age or a little younger than you, a more egalitarian relationship. I love young men. With age, men have a tendency to become less sensitive and more lascivious. Especially if they are facing the phantom of impotence."

Her boss let out a hearty, entertaining laugh. Elida was thinking to herself as she played with a small ceramic toucan that was on the table with her hands.

"Why are you so pensive all of a sudden?"

"I don't know; I was thinking about Federico. When I met him, he was fifty-two, and he was a sweet and tender man. No one has ever caressed me the way he did."

"That's the only thing that improves with age."

"What?"

"Their hands."

And she laughed again with that tone that frightened Elida a little.

"Although young men are no guarantee of anything," she added. "Instead of changing, many of them become more hardened in their positions. Machismo and homosexuality, which are a lot like one another, are more prevalent than ever. Just imagine, once I heard a young man say that if he had to choose, he'd much rather live with a caring and attentive man who was gay than with a bitter feminist."

Elida listened with some skepticism. She had a strange feeling that that woman was trying to pervert her, or at least take off her blindfold or open a window with a different view. Her boss must have sensed Elida's feelings and she tried to soften her tone.

"The things I'm saying may seem harsh to you. I have lived a long time; I'm forty-nine years old, and believe me, that's a long time. I have had to struggle too much to make a place for myself and to keep it. And, at the end of so much fighting, they've had to raise my fist in the air the way they do with boxing champions. And besides that, I'm not giving up."

The seriousness in her eyes, which were lost for an instant at the top of an araucaria tree, revealed a strong determination that was not free of fatigue.

After a pause, she looked at Elida and continued:

"You know that I'm supporting one of the Party's candidates in the primaries. It's probably not the best party and he's probably not the best candidate, but we have to plow with the oxen we have. That's another thing that we learn with age, to abandon utopias. I might be on the top of the ballot for a seat in the National Assembly. I'm really interested in the project that I talked to you about the other day. And I'm even more interested that you be there when I leave the Institute."

Elida thought that that was the missing piece of the puzzle.

"I understand."

"You might think that I'm an ambitious person, that I want to take advantage of you or something like that. Well, you're right, that's the way it is. I don't like lies or euphemisms. It's not enough to work and earn a living. We have to get involved in politics because politics gets involved in our lives. To be at the margin of power is like playing house."

"Maybe," Elida said with doubt, "I haven't made up my mind yet about that job. To tell the truth, I'm a little frightened."

"You have the skill to make this project a success and even more. The problem with women is that they get scared and stop at any obstacle they encounter. And the worst part is that there are many women who create their own obstacles when they don't run into any at all. We can't wait long Elida."

"I know. We'll talk about it Monday in your office, if that's okay with you. I have to go now. I told Andrés I'd meet him for lunch."

When she said goodbye to her boss, several words remained dancing in her head. While she waited for a taxi, she finally articulated the idea that was bursting to come out of her. To play house and to believe in fairy tales. When she was little, she envied adults; she wanted to be like them. And now that she was an adult, she still envied them.

"How did my boss grow so much?" she asked herself.

## Chapter Twenty-Two

### *The Shirt of a Happy Man*

What advantage was there in growing up? That was what Elida was thinking about when she entered the restaurant where Andrés was waiting for her. She saw him sitting in the back, next to a leafy palm tree and several enormous wicker baskets. The joint was decorated with antique irons, old sewing machines, and ancient indigenous clay pots. Brilliantly colored fruit was spread out on a counter that separated the restaurant from the bar.

A young woman with long blond hair was chatting with Andrés. When she saw Elida coming, she went away with a slight limp.

Andrés got up, kissed Elida on the cheek, very close to her lips, and seated her.

"What a pretty girl!"

"Yes, she's very special. I've known her for years," Andrés answered, giving the impression he wanted drop the subject.

It was the first time they were together outside his apartment. Elida seemed strange, as if she were naked, as if all of a sudden they were two strangers forced to recognize an intimacy that at that moment seemed remote.

Andrés, to the contrary, looked at her with delight—he was praising her blouse, her eye makeup, and the warm atmosphere of the restaurant— in complete control of the situation.

"It's chilly in here," Elida said.

"Chilly? When I'm near you, I never feel cold."

Elida smiled because she felt she had to. The obvious always made her suspicious.

"Is something wrong?" Andrés asked as he caressed Elida's hand.

"No, nothing... I just had a conversation with my boss."

"About your resignation?"

"Not exactly. We talked a little bit about everything. She has offered me a promotion, a position with a lot of responsibility."

"What about the salary?" Andrés asked as he pulled his hand away from hers.

"It's almost double. I don't know what to do. I'm not cut out for an administrative position. I'd have to travel all over the country, buy a car... I don't know; it will complicate my life; besides, I don't really know if I like the idea."

Andrés was thinking about it. What should he say? He decided to say what he really thought.

"That's right, peace of mind is worth its weight in gold."

"But it could also be fear, insecurity..."

"That's not it, at least not in my case," Andrés replied in a defensive tone that to Elida seemed out of place. "I don't like to complicate my life," he added. "I only do what I really want to do. I have a friend at work who is studying chemistry right now. I left the university a long time ago, but he's still there. He studies at night and works during the day. He moonlights whenever he can; he's building a home with a loan that he got from the government. All he talks about is his wife, his kids; all he thinks about is money, money... No fucking way, that's not a life."

Elida contemplated him in silence. She did not say so, but Andrés's friend sounded nicer to her than that unexpected language which Andrés had used.

A waiter came to the table and they placed their order: a Caesar salad, a bowl of onion soup, and chicken vol-au-vents. And to drink: draft beer.

"You can't live without money," Elida said, realizing the simplicity of her statement.

"You're right, what else can we do, but we don't have to kill ourselves. I've never really worried about money. I have enough for my expenses and that's good enough. Making money is the easiest thing in the world," Andrés added with confidence. "You can deal cocaine and you'll get rich in no time... or you can devote yourself to satisfying old gringas at night."

Andrés paused for a second to observe Elida's reaction, but he could not detect anything in her expression.

"But I'm not interested in that," he continued. "I like to have time for myself. I hate pressure."

Elida thought that Andrés was a person without aspirations. She was too. She remembered her boss and she sighed, disillusioned. Andrés looked at her again tenderly.

"Do you know the story *The Shirt of a Happy Man*?"

"No."

"Look, once upon a time there was a rich and powerful king who was very sick with sadness. His doctors didn't know how to cure him. They called the most famous wise men in the world, but nothing did any good. Finally, a wise man from the orient came. After examining the king, he said: your majesty will get well when he wears the shirt of a happy man. The king sent his messengers to look for that shirt. They went all over the kingdom asking everyone if they were happy, but all of them answered no. There was always something that prevented them from being happy.

The days and months passed, and the messengers returned to the palace empty handed. As they were crossing a mountain pass they came upon a man resting in the shade of a tree. They approached and asked him if he was a happy man. That guy, without taking his eyes off the clouds, answered yes, that he was a completely happy man. Unfortunately, he didn't own a shirt."

When he finished the story, Andrés let out a hearty laugh.

"Do you get it?"

Elida remained silent. She was about to ask him what the king did after that, but she understood that it did not matter and she said nothing.

"There is people like us, just like that, Elida. Happy and shirtless. The word "is" took Elida by surprise. She remembered Federico's obsession with correcting any grammar mistakes he heard. She continued to be silent and looked at Andrés with nostalgia, the way one looks at the past.

All of a sudden, a shrill voice shouted Andrés's name from the door. A spectacular black English-speaking woman approached them moving like a panther.

*"Hi, honey!"* she gave him a loud kiss on the cheek.

"Diana!" Andrés responded with controlled enthusiasm.

*"But, what are you doin' here? Today's the lunch at Rafa's."*

"I can't go, I'm already booked."

*"No kiddin'..."*

And without looking at Elida, she gave Andrés another kiss and left swinging her hips amidst the satisfied stares of the restaurant's other male customers.

"I didn't know you speak English."

"I lived in Los Angeles for a while."

"Really, when?"

"About fifteen years ago."

"What were you doing there, were you studying?"

"No, are you kidding. When I left the university, I went there to work for a while. I almost got married," he added with a laugh.

"Really," Elida asked with noticeable interest.

"A very fat gringa woman with tons of money. She had a beautiful face. She was crazy about me. She thought I was her authentic *Latin lover.* You know how gringos are crazy about anything that's 'real'!"

"So, you were a *real Latin lover*?"

As she asked him this, she remembered having read something about there being two kinds of Don Juans: those that pursue woman and those that are pursued by them; the last group was indubitably the most dangerous and devastating. Which group did Andrés belong to?

> *There was a crazy, crazy time in my life, I was around twenty-five, those were ardent, wild years, with more than fifty girls in less than a year, it was like being in paradise without dying. Of course, there was no time to complete files for my dossier, I could barely keep track of them, only my Brazilian friend outdid me, he told me he had done ninety girls the last time we spoke, but he was at the university, and that was his advantage. Those gringas were divine, I imagined all of them with Playboy Bunny ears and all of the gringo boys with Mickey Mouse ones.*

"I did the best I could," he answered evasively. But the real lady killer was a midget, the son of a Mexican woman and Greek man. His face wasn't small, just his legs and arms. He was seventeen years old, with long, black eyelashes. Those eyelashes swept every woman off her feet. Apparently, his eyelashes weren't the only thing he had that was thick and long..."

Andrés noticed that Elida had started to eat her salad again and he smiled with a little regret, but enjoying at the same time the atavistic pleasure of being scandalous.

Elida did not take her eyes off her plate, trying, as best she could, to put up with the stench of low-class machismo that she hated so much.

"And that girl, is she from Los Angeles?"

"Diana, no she's Jamaican."

"Oh."

She remained silent until she had finished her salad.

"Why are you so serious? Don't you have a sense of humor? Smile, laugh!"

Elida took the opportunity to ask a passing waiter for a cup of coffee.

It was the second time that day that someone had pointed that out to her. They were right: she was too serious. She could not adjust well to the latest fashion that privileged laughter as a new lifestyle. The laugh that smoothes over everything and makes the person using it look sexy. Julio Iglesias fell in love with Giannina because she made him laugh; Margaret Thatcher loved to talk with Ronald Reagan because she was amused by his jokes; in *The Name of the Rose*, laughter is the cause of a murder; Durrell said that the thing women adore the most, after sex, of course, is laughing, and that is why the voluptuous Jessica married Roger Rabbit. In the old days only kings had buffoons. Nowadays, all citizens have a democratic right to laugh, the civic duty to laugh. You should not be sad or serious, that is the new commandment of this incredulous age.

Andrés's caress distracted her.

"Of course, I like to laugh. Once I fell in love with a guy because of the way he laughed."

"So, what you like is to see people laugh."

"Maybe, especially when their laughing coincides with mine. It's a special kind of communication, in a certain way, a profound one."

"That happens to me when I'm having sex."

"What a surprise, you men only have sex on your mind!"

"Here we are back on stereotypes again. I know a lot of woman who are like that. Sex is the most profound form of communication between two people."

"Perhaps."

"Why do you always say perhaps?"

Elida laughed and Andrés moved close to her to whisper in her ear:

"You're beautiful when you laugh."

Without paying attention to him and taking him by surprise, she asked him if they could get the check.

Deciding who would pay was always a serious matter for Andrés. He acted according to the economic status of the woman as well as his own expectations with respect to their relationship. As a general rule of thumb, he avoided paying the bill by himself, just as he refused to give gifts or make any other gesture that placed him anywhere near the role of a provider. Skillfully, biding his time, he waited for Elida's reaction.

"Let's go Dutch."

"If you wish," he responded without showing any emotion but very pleased inside.

When they left the restaurant, they walked slowly, side by side. Elida did not fail to notice the fleeting glances that Andrés adeptly directed at other women as they passed by. His eyes glided like the fine brush strokes of a painter. Elida was not jealous, a little envious perhaps, she wanted to be observed or look at others that way.

She remembered what she had said to her boss about polygamy when they discussed Andrés's visits. Indubitably, having a lot of women confers great status on a man in our society. They cannot escape that pressure. It comes from the ancient custom of polygamy. Only the rich and powerful had harems. In those days, a man could live with as many women as he could support. Nowadays, if you're not careful, her boss had told her, they are the "kept" ones without losing their status.

She was thinking about the kind of reputation a woman who has several men acquires, when, all of a sudden, Andrés took her by the arm.

"Let's go dancing tonight!" he said with lots of enthusiasm. "We can go to the Parking Lot, or to Your Diamonds, before the neighbors have their way and shut them down. They have fabulous music."

Seeing him move his shoulders, as if he were dancing a mambo, made Elida remember several titles of sensual and denigrating songs about women: *Whatever the man wants, Black Salomé, Juana the Cuban Girl, Shake that thing, My tush*, and she said: "No thanks."

"Don't you like to dance?"

"Not much, that's not my kind of music."

"What kind of music do you like? Don't tell me you like gringo music."

Elida remembered George Michael's latest song.

"Some of it," Elida replied timidly.

"Michael Jackson, for example, with his hysterical woman's voice... Did you know he gets hormone shots so he won't lose his voice?"

"Well, he wouldn't be the first one," Elida answered, recovering her serenity. "Have you heard about the castrated singers?"

"Castrated?" he asked, feigning a shudder.

"When women weren't allowed to sing in church, they castrated boys so they could sing like women. They were greatly sought after by Popes and they earned a lot of money. The last one died in Rome sixty years ago."

"That's amazing!" Andrés replied. "And how do you know so much? Do you read *Reader's Digest* every month?"

"I don't read *Reader's Digest*. I don't appreciate bad jokes," she answered sharply.

Andrés put his arm around her shoulders.

"Are you mad at me?" the wolf in sheep's clothing asked her in an affectionate tone.

"Not at all."

"Then why don't we go dancing tonight?"

"No, I'd rather go home."

"To my house?"

"No, to mine."

"And what are you going to do on a Sunday afternoon locked up in your house?"

"Think, for example. I have to give my boss an answer."

Andrés took his arm off her and sighed. Do I have to play the victim again? Andrés asked himself why this woman had to be so difficult.

"Okay, I'll take you home."

"That's not necessary, it's not far away. You can still go to your friend's party."

"I'm not interested in any party now, Elida. And besides," he paused, "today makes a week that we have known each other."

Elida looked at him, surprised by his sudden seriousness, discovering again the sweetness of his gray eyes.

When they reached the apartment buildings, Andrés put his arm around her waist.

"After you're done thinking, call me. We can talk; we'll order a pizza and beer. I would like that very much..."

Before leaving, she kissed him. As she climbed the stairs, she thought Andrés was a puzzle. If she wanted to love him, she had no choice but to accept the game and to use every single piece.

## Chapter Twenty-Three

### *Passionate Diana*

He had provoked it. At least foreseen it: He knew when he took that girl to his house that Elida could show up at any moment.

He even knew, at the very moment he was making plans with Elida, that he would go to Rafa's party, that some woman would fall into his trap and that they would end up in bed. He had a vague notion of this when he had asked her. For this reason, he spoke with that strange, malignant intensity that Elida could not turn down.

And now they were there. He saw her looking upwards, searching for him. Andrés watched her from the window in the corner. And then he looked at the eyes of the smiling dark woman waiting for him on his couch. He remembered himself in earlier days.

Even as a young man, Andrés had had the bad habit of betrayal. He loved to escape from one woman so he could melt into the arms of another. He found it intoxicating. The first time he cheated on a woman was when he was having an adolescent romance with a friend from school. The betrayal was possible because he loved her a lot. How could we betray those we do not love? It had to be that way: unjustified, unjust, gratuitous, a gratifying breaking of words and limits.

That first time left an indelible mark on Andrés. He always did it because he had the tendency to betray, he was addicted to the incomparable aphrodisiac of guilt.

For a long time, he ran from woman to woman with the eagerness of a dog and the speed of a hummingbird, lost in his labyrinth of lies and promises, knowing neither the origin of those escapes nor the pressing need which they met.

However, that night, perhaps because he was in his forties or who-knows-why, he had the impression that he was doing something really stupid. He observed Elida, he heard the doorbell ring three times, and when he saw her walk away, he went back to the couch on the verge of feeling terrible.

Diana was sitting there with her enormous, shiny thighs, waiting for him. File number three, he thought to himself.

From the time he got to Rafa's, she had thrown her arms around his neck shouting how happy she was that he was there. He felt as pampered as a trophy.

*"She isn't here yet,"* she whispered to him in English.

*"Who?"*

*"Rafa's French girl."*

Most of the people were in the garden. There were few women. He could make out Rafa and several of his friends in the midst of the smoke from the grill. A short time later the honking of a car horn was heard and he saw Rafa head for the door like a gust of wind.

A group of men immediately formed a tight circle. When that blond doll appeared, in a very short black miniskirt and a tight, low-cut lace blouse, every man present opened his mouth and became silent. They watched in astonishment when, with her *I-don't-know-any-Spanish smile*, she shook their hands one by one.

When she finished greeting them, she sat down—with her back very straight and always smiling—on the edge of a chair. As if obeying a formal command, when she crossed her legs, all eyes present stared at the tiny white buttocks that emerged from the edge of her miniskirt. One of Andrés's gay friends, who usually had something sarcastic to say, said to him softy:

"Look how they open their eyes, you son-of-a-bitch. It's because of their erections; their skin is so tight they can't even shut their eyelids."

Andrés let out a loud laugh, even though he had already heard the joke and despite the impression that the blond had also left on him.

"Where did Rafa get that piece of candy?"

"She's the niece of the cultural attaché from the embassy. She looks seventeen, but she's really twenty-six. She came here to study Spanish, and Rafa is going to be her teacher."

"She's not bad at all..."

"No, she's not bad at all. She even makes me feel like a lesbian; what do you think of that?"

They laughed and contemplated with aloofness Rafa's attempts to protect the girl from the cloud of marauders. He took her by the hand, placed his arm over her shoulders, around her waist, without breaking physical or visual contact with her for even a second.

It was after seven when the music started to play. Diana, who had not let him out of her sight all evening long, approached him like a feline.

*"Wanna dance?"*

*"I'd rather we leave and go to my place."*

He said it without thinking it over, and then he could not take it back. It was not the first time that he had "had" to make love in order not to leave a bad impression because he had committed himself, so that no one would talk about it. Once a certain point is reached, a man cannot say no. He remembered Elida and the stereotypes. As she would say, "maybe" the time had arrived to end another form of slavery and to do what he really wanted to do.

Diana's body burned his skin. He observed her mouth, which looked like a juicy star apple, and thought that he might just change his mind about her later on. It is always better to leave a door open. When the doorbell was ringing, he was thinking of telling her: "It's my neighbors; I forgot that I have to get together with them tonight. If you want, I can walk you home. I'm sorry Diana. Can I call you tomorrow?"

But when Diana began to rub his pants above the knee and showed him the pink tip of her tongue, Andrés forgot about everything else.

## Chapter Twenty-Four

### *The Color of the Lens*

Elida entered the apartment without kissing or touching him. An indefinite space had established itself between them, a kind of no man's land.

Andrés had decided that he would not be the one to bring up what had happened the night before. Nevertheless, he was going over in his mind how he would justify his behavior.

Elida looked him in the eyes.

"Why didn't you answer last night? You were home, I saw you in the window."

"I was busy."

"At least you could have told me."

"I couldn't because I was really tied up."

"You were with a woman."

"That's my business," Andrés answered impatiently.

"If we have a relationship, it's also my business, isn't it?"

"We've already gone over that, Elida. There's no reason to belabor the point."

Andrés paced back and forth in the living room. This time he was having more trouble dealing with this kind of conflict. That's what I get for getting involved with a neighbor, he thought, too close for comfort, too much control.

He thought about expressing his anger openly, but he did not want Elida to leave his apartment with bitter feelings. Knowing how to end a relationship was an art he had cultivated with great care. Pablo Neruda was right when he said, "Love is so brief and oblivion so eternal!"

He had encountered in almost every woman he had known the powerful tendency towards *continuism*, an inertia towards the infinite that he had learned to break with the least amount of pain, with quick, repeated disappointments or with spectacular performances, depending on the case. He did not like the idea of accumulating a past full of rancorous women. But above all else, he realized that he did not want to lose Elida.

He suffered a rare attack of sincerity and suddenly turned around to face her.

"One of the most difficult things to accept about women is their possessiveness, that desire that a man's commitment to them be forever. They show up at any time of any day and expect us to be waiting for them, willing to welcome them, to drop everything in order to devote ourselves completely to them. It's as if they look upon every man as a child they can manipulate."

Elida looked at him with surprise because of the theoretical twist that Andrés had tried give to their conversation. He was the one who had invited her into his life. After a moment of silence, staring at the ashtray, Elida murmured "I don't have children," in the manner one who is resigned to talking about something else would.

"That doesn't matter; it's the maternal paradigm that counts, even if a woman doesn't have any children. You're all genetically predisposed to possess someone and that predisposition is projected onto any relationship. We men have to fight to maintain our own identity, our freedom."

"Is that genetic too?" she asked.

Andrés looked at Elida, who was still staring at the ashtray. He sat down next to her. Her long, fine hair interrupted his thoughts for a moment. Jealousy also has its tender side.

"Women are always a double-edged sword. They bring us happiness and take it away at the same time."

"I'm not saying that that's the case with me," Elida stated, "but, in general terms, how is it possible that the desire to love a man forever and ever could provoke so much rejection? It is precisely that timeless, gratuitous dimension that makes love so beautiful. What use is there in loving if it's not forever?"

"What I care about, what really concerns me, is not the ending, not whether love is forever or if it's going to end. What really matters to me is the happiness of each and every moment."

Elida let out a long sigh. It seemed to her that they had reached a point of agreement in their disagreement.

"I don't think men are capable of loving the way women do."

"Bullshit!" Andrés smiled. "Don't tell me that you're going to come out with that recalcitrant feminism now. Do you agree with those lesbians?"

"I had never thought about it that way, but probably the only person that can fully understand a woman is another woman. And it must be the same for you men. At heart, there's not much difference between your lifestyle and that of a promiscuous homosexual."

Andrés looked attentively at her.

"I'm not promiscuous. And much less a homosexual," he added sharply.

He got up and lit a cigarette with the gesture of one turning the page after reading the last word of a chapter in a book. Elida noticed this, and she tried to stay on the same topic.

"Have you ever had a homosexual encounter?"

Andrés thought to himself that it was not wise to tell a woman you have had homosexual relations at some time in the past. Much less at this point in time. At most, one can tell a story from the distant past, about early temptation and struggle, and burning interest, but one that makes it perfectly clear that the feminine gender garnered final victory. And that is what he told Elida from the bottom of his heart. She listened to his story not knowing whether to believe him or not.

With her attention still focused on a spot on the coffee table, she remembered the idea that she had just expressed: complete understanding between two women.

Right then she remembered Amalia: a limitless game of identities, fusion, and total affection, forever. At least that is the way it appeared. That is what they said to each other then, in the first longing of adolescence, the awakening of affection, their interest in beauty, to discover together the unending introspection, the severe criticism of adults, the power of their own reason to understand the world, inventing secret codes that only they understood. “I don’t know any Elida.” Like her father, like Federico, like so many other relationships that had to die, now Amalia was also lost forever, dead, with the same cold tone that the dead must use when they speak. “I don’t know any Elida.” She remembered her friend’s green eyes, always smiling, and then she tried to imagine her, sitting or perhaps standing, without her green eyes, without memories, with rigor mortis in her voice.

Maybe it’s better this way, she thought, with no ties, no prince, and no fairy godmother. Just Elida riding on top of her pumpkin.

Andrés’s gentle voice, a caress on her back, his eyes like cotton candy, the unmistakable tone of his desire.

Why not? Elida asked herself, why not accept that only the present exists, if they can do it and they’re happy, why not me, an infantile and perverse voice kept repeating over and over again, why not accept this tender moment, the bodies of two strangers pretending that they really love each other, melted together in their own selfishness, searching for a few moments of ecstasy, because pleasure is possible in this way.

Elida turned around and smiled in a way that surprised Andrés.

“I was thinking about you, my love, about how wonderful it is to be with you.”

And as she embraced his body with a primitive strength, as she kissed him anxiously until she could not breath, Elida thought that what she was thinking could be true: that she loved him at that moment, that she desired him, that it did not matter what happened later, that it was easy to tell those lies that she wanted to be true, that perhaps all she had to do was say things for them to be true for that moment, with no transcendence.

It was a matter of choosing another lens and seeing the world in another color. Of putting on the mask that protects freedom. To use, the way they do, the empty language of promises that they know are false, the discourse of seduction. And like a bizarre abscess, a decision flowed out naturally, she would accept her boss’s job offer.

After they made love, Andrés forgot about his habitual somnolent abandonment to observe attentively Elida’s face. A strange mystery had taken possession of her. Though she was still Elida, she was herself in a different way.

She tried but could not discover what it was about her that had changed. She relived the enigma of their encounter that night by the train, the wolf woman, the howling Cinderella. Andrés felt the same perplexity, the same impotence of one who has lost all sense of direction on a dark street.

While they embraced each other, he had tried to look into Elida's eyes, but Elida had kept her eyes closed. Her distant sighs were no longer meant for him as they had been on other occasions—when they had wounded his fantasy and desire—but flew away and were lost in the luminous, crystalline raindrops.

Nor did she cuddle up beside him to become smaller in his arms. Nor did she sigh when, after they were exhausted, he kissed her. She neither smiled nor said a single word.

Andrés felt lonelier than ever. For that reason, when she tried to get up to go to the bathroom, he tried to keep her at his side. And when he did so, he forgot all his do's and don'ts, his fears, his old suspicions, about exploring the terrain and consequences, and he said to her, "Why don't you spend the night here?"

Elida smiled and, without saying a word, she disappeared behind the bathroom door.

Several long minutes passed and Elida reappeared completely dressed with her makeup on. Andrés had a foreboding feeling when he saw her, is she leaving me? Is she leaving me forever?

He approached her slowly. Her coldness overwhelmed him; the delightful freshness was gone; now a solid space separated them.

"My little pumpkin, don't go away," he whispered in her ear. "Stay with me tonight."

Elida looked at him. All at once she remembered the "lines" of women, his endless "visitors," his refusal to commit himself to a relationship, his pretentious language and uncouth expressions, his tendency to accept mediocrity effortlessly, his lack of energy to fight, at the very bottom of everything his loneliness, his fear of life, hidden beneath his compulsive sexual activity.

Elida felt no hostility towards him or sadness for him.

She had already given up on her idea of a dream man, because he does not exist. She had also renounced the impossible job of turning a man into her perfect prince. Now, she could only try to understand and accept them as they are, as they come, like Andrés.

You can take them or leave them, she thought to herself. Had she become superficial or had she simply acquired a new sense of humor?

"No, Andrés. I'm leaving and I'm not coming back."

"But Elida, why? Don't we get along fine...? I love you," he told her with a pathetic look in his eyes.

It was the first time that Elida heard him saying those words, the first time she saw him cry. A long time ago, when she would see a grown man cry, it was heart wrenching. But then, when she learned that men cry just as much and almost as often as women, it no longer made an impression on her.

She looked at him with the tenderness of farewells and said to him:

"Goodbye, Andrés. Thanks for everything. You've really given me a lot!"

"Okay, as you wish," he replied softly.

She went down the stairs, out into the street, and took a deep breath. When she reached the first corner, she turned around to look back. There was Andrés, raising his arm, so far away!

She returned his farewell gesture and disappeared in the streets of the city, a city of new streets through her new lens.

As she walked, Elida felt a strange combination of heaviness and weightlessness. Her high heels dug into the ground with force; they drilled it, leaving tracks behind her. A real person had passed through there, not a ghost or shadow; Elida, a woman who moved about lightly, weightlessly, without chains or ties: her feet and arms felt light, the movement of her body inside her clothing, conscious of the harmonious movement of her hips as she walked, without hiding or holding anything back, her long hair flowing free in the wind, receiving the glances of men the way the moon does, fearlessly and without shame, with delight, with an extraordinary pleasure of being admired and then walking on by, the unequaled pleasure of feeling like a woman, having within her power the key to understanding men and accepting them the way they are, without idealizing dreams, without angry withdrawals, without having to renounce them, to look them straight in the eyes, as equals, and if possible, to fall in love again but in a different way, and to be happier than ever.

Elida felt an immense desire to howl, but she smiled, a new smile that changed her face, and she no longer needed to be younger or more beautiful to be happy, because she could be herself no more than she was at that moment, and that is the greatest beauty and the greatest happiness, at thirty-three, the age of the chosen men and women, the energy of her small steel core finally freed, affirming life, happiness, and a new way of loving.

What would her next love be like? Blond, dark, young, older, a traditional *"macho"* or a *garçon fragile*?

What would Federico say to her when she went to see him without any resentment, the most carefree smile in the world on her face, and asked him: "What's up? How have you been?

What illness would her mother contract when she told her to stop looking for a husband for her, that she had lost all interest in trapping a man to end up with him in a jail cell or an insane asylum?

And last but not least, what would Andrés think if he knew that he was going to be the first entry in a love diary that she planned to inaugurate that very night?

*The translators express their deep gratitude to Sharon Heller and Linda Berrón for their assistance in revising the translation. Their thoughtful suggestions contributed greatly towards improving the final version of this novel.*

# *Afterword*

Linda Berrón's *The Dossier* performs a profound critique of the construction of gender identities, the sentimental education that sustains them and the disenchantment, failure, and loneliness that are produced when one expects the "other" to fill the shortcomings of a social and sexual ideology that constructs human beings as opposites and incomplete, in which the male is the one who has the power to name things.

The Dossier subverts this cultural order. The novel begins with the personal reflections of Andrés, a man who has centered his life around the apprenticeship of seduction. He seeks to collect women; they represent a trophy for his masculinity, thus the need for files that remind him of his worth as a promiscuous male. He is forty years old, he experiences loneliness and he cannot even name that sensation that suddenly arrives and escapes his comprehension. He does not possess the symbolic elements to do so. The fact that a female author can construct a male protagonist and penetrate his subjectivity to dismantle it, is original. Generally, it is a male author who, when constructing his feminine protagonist, translates an experience which is not his own but rather one that expresses his desires, fears, and fantasies with respect to women, mysterious beings who, no matter how empathetic he is, escape his comprehension.

Linda Berrón subverts the aforementioned state of affairs; as a creator she penetrates the mirror that that subjective masculinity provides her in order to, like Alice through the Looking Glass, expose it from the inside and destroy it. For this reason, female readers, who encounter Elida, a woman who is searching for the prince promised in fairy tales —"a powerful, tender man who would take charge of her life," "intelligent and sensitive," "one capable of overcoming the contradictions and salvaging love" — do not read the novel as affirming the condition of otherness with which they have been "educated." Instead, they encounter an intelligent woman, who after her relationship with Andrés, is capable of standing on her own two feet and walking with joy towards personal autonomy, for only she can take care of herself and create her own dreams. In the novel, Elida is not punished for her efforts; on the contrary, she is the winner. Andrés is the one who loses and he does not even know it; he persists in hunting for new prey in an attempt to fill his emptiness.

*The Dossier* is not a novel that is directed solely at women. For male readers, it offers new symbolic elements that will allow them to name their maladies, to reflect and question that construction of masculinity that does not satisfy them either, thus offering them the possibility of establishing more satisfactory relationships, of interdependency, with their equals.

*Dr. Consuelo Meza Márquez*
*Autonomous University of Aguascalientes, Mexico*

www.ingramcontent.com/pod-product-compliance
Lightning Source LLC
Chambersburg PA
CBHW030532310726
48979CB00010B/1894/J

* 9 7 8 1 6 1 0 1 2 0 3 8 8 *